To Bonnie, Mac, and Barb.

HECTOR

The bell rang. Fourth period was over. Hector Turcio tossed his books into his book bag. Wednesdays were always tough. Dr. Miller's labs often ran past the bell.

He burst through the side door and walked quickly to the parking lot. He didn't have to search for his car. He knew right where he'd left it. Same spot every day. Backed in against the far fence. But even if he hadn't parked in his usual spot, he could pick it out.

The black Lexus ES 350 was the hottest car in Capital Central High School's parking lot.

Leaning against it, trying to use the side mirror as she put on lipstick, was Jacleen Thompson. The hottest girl at Cap Central.

Cap Central kids didn't have the money for

nice cars. The school was located in the Northeast quadrant of Washington, D.C. Although people with money were moving in and fixing up houses, most of the kids who attended Cap Central were from families who didn't have much. Those who were lucky enough to have a car mostly had beaters—their own family's cast-offs or junkers bought cheap.

No one else had a Lexus. Or anything even close. And his was as sweet a ride inside as it looked outside. Fully loaded. GPS. Rear back-up camera. Leather seats.

A car like that should make anyone happy. Especially someone as crazy about cars as Hector was. Just as a girl like Jacleen should make any guy happy. She was tall, with perfect skin, long processed hair, and huge dark eyes. Jacleen wanted to be a model. She was pretty enough to make it. In fact, she had already gotten some jobs.

Hector knew he was the envy of most of the boys at Cap Central. They'd be surprised to know how miserable he felt.

The deal he'd made with Dez Arnold for the use of the Lexus was turning into a nightmare.

One he couldn't see his way out of. And to be honest? Hector knew that without the car, Jacleen would be gone.

She pressed herself against him in a hug. "Hey, baby, I looked for you everywhere this morning," she cooed. "Where were you hiding?"

"I was around," he said.

In spite of himself, he was thrilled at being so close to Jacleen.

"I missed you," Jacleen said. Her face was so close to his that Hector could smell her lipstick. "I wanted to make sure you were coming back to Cap Cent after your Tech classes so we could spend the afternoon together."

"I'll be back," Hector said. He was embarrassed that his voice sounded funny. But Jacleen always seemed to have that effect on him.

" 'Cause I need you to take me to the nail spa after school. I want to get my nails done," Jacleen said. "Brennay and Zakia too."

Hector's heart fell. Just once, he wished Jacleen would suggest spending time together that didn't involve him having to drive her somewhere. And he didn't look forward to having Brennay Baxter and Zakia Johnson in the car. When the three girls were together, he was invisible.

"I have to pick up my grandmother from the dialysis clinic at four thirty," he said. "But I can drive you before that."

He heard footsteps from behind.

"Sorry I'm late," Marley Macomb said.

Hector turned around. Marley attended classes at D.C. Vocational Technical Academy with Hector in the afternoons. Hector studied automotive science, while Marley studied computer technology.

Hector pulled away from Jacleen and used his remote so that Marley could get into the car.

"I can't believe you're friends with her," Jacleen whispered in his ear. "She's so … rough."

Marley looked like someone whose family didn't have much money. Her clothes weren't fashionable—or even new—and sometimes her hair needed a little work. She worked long hours at the Kwik n'Carry, a convenience store on Benning Road. But Marley was funny and smart. She and Hector had become good friends on their daily rides to Tech. Hector didn't like hearing Jacleen criticize her.

"She's okay," Hector said. "Anyway, I'll see you later, okay? I'm gonna be late if I don't get going,"

Jacleen kissed him on the mouth.

"I'll be waiting, sugar," she whispered. She pressed herself against him. "Any chance you could pick us up when our nails are done? After you drop off your grandma, of course?"

Seemed like everyone he knew needed rides lately. Hector was glad to help out his grandmother and happy to give Marley a ride to Tech. As for Jacleen? He'd drive her anywhere if it meant she'd continue to stand so close.

"Sure," he said.

"You're the best," she gushed. "I'll see you later, okay?"

Hector watched as she walked away.

He knew this came at a price. The things Dez Arnold wanted him to do were becoming dangerous. So far, Hector hadn't broken any laws. At least, he didn't think he had. But he had seen things going on at Dez Arnold's car repair shop that he knew couldn't be legal.

Arnold had given him the car in exchange for helping out around the shop on weekends.

The deal seemed perfect. On-the-job experience, plus the use of a great car. For free.

And then he learned what Dez Arnold was really up to.

It wasn't fixing cars or doing oil changes.

Hector got in the car and started it up. He knew the right thing to do was to give the car back and stay as far away from Dez Arnold as possible. But life with a car was so much better than life without one.

Especially *this* car.

The appeal was just too great to give it up.

As Hector found out, the car wasn't free after all. The only question left was how high a price would he end up paying.

CHAPTER 2

MARLEY

Marley waited until Hector headed down Eleventh Street before she said anything.

"So where does the princess need her carriage to take her today?" she asked. She knew how she sounded. But honestly, she could not understand how Hector could be so blind.

Jacleen was using him. No other way to explain it. A girl with Jacleen Thompson's looks actually hot for Hector? The thought was enough to make Marley laugh.

"Nowhere," Hector said. "She just wants to hang out."

Marley chuckled. She knew he was lying. "Because she's *so* hot for you, right?" she said. "And if you didn't have a car ..." she teased.

"Leave it alone," Hector said gruffly. "Not

like I see you turning down my ride," he added meanly.

Marley was surprised. Hector had spoken sharply to her before, but not about giving her a ride. His words hurt.

Because they were true.

Marley turned to look out the side window. Without a ride, she would have to take two buses to get to her afternoon classes at Tech on Martin Luther King Jr. Avenue in Southeast. The trip could take up to hour, depending on traffic. It was also expensive.

Although D.C. students could ride the bus in the morning and after school for free, the ride between Cap Central and Tech in the middle of the day cost close to two dollars. Ten dollars per week was more than Marley felt she could ask her mom to pay.

Before this year, she hadn't known Hector. It was impossible to know everyone at such a large high school. They'd met at the bus stop at the corner of Bladensburg Road and H Street on the first day that classes started at Tech. They chatted until they got to their stop a few blocks from the Tech campus.

It was a pain to travel between the two schools. But Marley felt that the training she was receiving was worth the inconvenience. Already, the computer classes she took at Tech had enabled her to help others with IT issues. She could repair most computers, handle software issues, and save less-skilled computer users from catastrophe.

Her dream was to work for the government in cybersecurity. The intense training she got at Tech would help her find a starting job in the field. Her plan was to save money while she worked until she could afford to go to college.

Everything improved when Hector got the Lexus. Marley would meet him in the high school's parking lot for the ride to Southeast. After class, Hector dropped her at her apartment or at the Kwik n'Carry if she had to work.

And lately, she was working more. Marley's family was living on the edge. Her mother had lost her job with the D.C. government after having twins. The babies had some health issues. By the time they were well, she couldn't find any affordable childcare for them or Marley's four-year-old sister.

There were months when the only money coming in was what Marley earned working at the store. Her paycheck wasn't enough to cover all the bills. Her mother got food from food banks and other places, but often they went to bed hungry.

That was one of the many reasons she resented Jacleen. Jacleen looked like someone for whom life's biggest tragedy was a broken fingernail. When she was around Jacleen, Marley was conscious of her unstyled hair and old clothes.

Marley hadn't told Hector how close her family was to disaster. She always thanked him for giving her a ride without telling him how desperately she needed his help. If she had to take buses back to the Kwik n'Carry in Northeast after her Tech classes, she would have lost at least an hour of work.

He had never indicated that he minded giving her a ride.

"I've told you before, I want to help pay for gas," Marley said. Her voice shook a little. She had offered numerous times to give him gas money. He'd always said no.

"Nah, it's all good," Hector said. "Sorry. Got a lot on my mind I guess."

"What's up?" Marley asked.

Hector just shook his head. "Nothing I feel like talking about," he answered.

Marley wondered what was troubling him. She felt completely comfortable around Hector. She had thought he felt the same way. She thought they trusted each other enough to talk about anything.

Well, almost anything. There were two subjects that were off limits.

The first was how he'd managed to get the Lexus.

Marley knew where the car had come from. Each time they had sprinted from the bus to Tech, they had seen it parked at the curb in front of an auto repair shop. The car was a beauty. They had both admired it whenever they passed it.

The auto repair shop, however, was another story. It never seemed to have much business. The same two cars were always parked out front with their hoods open. Either the mechanics were so bad that they couldn't fix whatever was wrong with the cars, or the cars were just props to make the repair shop look like it was legitimate.

A few weeks after the start of school, Hector hadn't been at the bus stop outside of Cap Central. As Marley waited to catch the bus, the Lexus pulled up beside her. The passenger-side window came down. Hector leaned over the seat.

"Get in," he said.

Marley did. She looked at him curiously.

"I'm borrowing it," he said before she even asked. "In exchange for working at that garage on weekends."

"They actually fix cars there?" Marley had asked incredulously.

"I guess," he said.

It wasn't the answer Marley had been expecting. "You don't know for sure?" she said.

"No, I'm sure," Hector said. "Of course they fix cars. That's what I'm gonna do there on weekends. Help with repairs and stuff."

By that time, Marley knew Hector well enough to know he was lying. Or if not lying, at least not telling her everything.

"Whatever," she said.

From then on, Hector shut down whenever the subject of the car came up. After a while, Marley knew not to ask.

The other subject that was guaranteed to make Hector snap at her?

Jacleen.

CHAPTER 3

HECTOR

As soon as the words were out of his mouth, Hector regretted it. And saying he was sorry wouldn't fix things. He knew his words had hurt Marley. He already felt lousy about himself. Hurting her made him feel even worse.

And she hadn't said anything, really. Just voiced what he was already thinking about Jacleen.

Marley had a way of zeroing in on the very thing he was feeling uncomfortable about. She would ask him questions that showed she wasn't fooled by his half-truths. They could talk about most everything. He had come to consider her his closest friend. But there were two subjects he wouldn't discuss with her. The first was Jacleen.

And the second was the Lexus.

He could remember when he first saw the car. It was during his first week at Tech. He was still getting used to his busy schedule. He went to Cap Central in the morning. Then he attended DC Vocational Technical Academy in the afternoon.

When he'd signed up to take classes at the Tech Academy, he knew the schedule was going to be tough. But it was worth it. All he'd ever wanted to be was a mechanic. He was willing to do whatever it took to achieve his dream. Even if it meant taking two Metro buses just to get to class.

He'd met Marley at the bus stop on the first day of school. They'd immediately become friends. She was the first girl he ever met who was as driven as he was to achieve a goal. Her passion for computers was a match for his passion for cars. The two of them rode the buses together and walked as fast as they could from the bus stop to Tech. Even so, they barely made it in time for the start of class.

As they raced down Martin Luther King Jr.

Avenue, they both commented on the beautiful Lexus parked in front of a run-down auto repair shop. The car was out of place for the neighborhood. Hector wondered what it would be like to drive a car that nice. He vowed that some day when he owned his own garage, his own car would shine like the Lexus did.

Since he passed it every day, Hector started paying attention to the garage. It was a large building. But it had only two bays. There was a driveway that led around back, so Hector wondered if maybe there were more bays in the rear.

Two cars were always in front of the bays with their hoods up. Occasionally, Hector saw some guys in jumpsuits who looked like they might be mechanics. But they never seemed to be working on the cars out front.

A few weeks after school started, Marley wasn't there. Hector commuted to Tech by himself. As he walked past the garage, a guy in a nice suit came out.

"Son, I see you eyeing my car as you walk by each day," he said.

Hector backed up a step and put up his

hands. "Mister, I'm eyeing your car only because it looks like a sweet ride," he said. "I'm not looking for trouble."

The guy threw his head back and laughed. "I didn't think you were gonna take my car," he said. "I was just wondering if you ever thought about working in a garage. Anybody who drools over a car they way I see you drooling over mine must know cars pretty well."

Hector relaxed. "Actually, I come by here every day because I go to Tech to learn how to be a mechanic," he said. "So, yeah. I think about working in a garage. Pretty much all afternoon!"

The older man looked at him thoughtfully. "You go to Tech, huh? Used to go there myself back in the day. Woody Woodbine still teach there?"

Hector laughed. "He's still there," he said. "We call him the Little Dictator."

The guy laughed. "Nothing much changed there," he said. "When I went to Tech, they wanted us to get real-life experience. That still the case?"

Hector nodded. "Yeah. Woody talks about it all the time."

"So maybe we could work something out,"

the man said. "Think you might want to do some work for me? In exchange for, say, being able to drive the Lexus."

Hector couldn't believe what he was hearing. "Mister, there's *nothing* I wouldn't do for the chance to drive that car!"

"A true gearhead," the guy said with a laugh. "Well, for starters, how about you quit calling me Mister. I'm Dez. Dez Arnold." He stuck out his hand.

"Hector Turcio," Hector said, shaking his hand.

"Well, Hector, I have a lot of stuff that needs to get done. But my mechanics don't feel like doing it. Sweeping up, stocking shelves, other jobs too. We do a lot of, well, custom work. Specialty stuff, shall we say. Interested?"

"Are you kidding? Yeah!" Hector answered happily.

Later, when he told Marley about the conversation, she focused on the one part he wasn't sure about.

"What did he mean by 'custom work'?" she'd asked.

Hector wasn't sure. But he didn't want to tell her that he didn't know. "You know, stuff for customers," he said, trying to sound like he knew what he was talking about.

"I *don't* know, actually," she had said. "And what about the 'specialty stuff'? What does that mean?" she asked.

At that point, he got angry. "Quit dissing my new car and my job!" he'd snapped. "It's custom stuff. Out of the ordinary jobs, okay? Truth is, you sound jealous!"

"Really?" Marley had answered. She sounded more amused than angry. "Jealous, huh? I think the place looks suspicious, that's all. I don't actually think they're working on cars at all. You need to watch yourself so you don't get sucked into something illegal."

Hector was so angry he said some things he shouldn't have.

It had taken them a few days to get back to their usual friendly talk.

Hector now wished he'd listened to her. Instead, all he had focused on was that he could work in a garage and drive a Lexus.

He knew now that he was in way over his head. The fear he felt made him quick to lash out. He hadn't meant to snap at Marley. Of course he didn't mind giving her a ride to Tech.

Her only fault was being right about Dez Arnold. And it worried him.

MARLEY

Despite Hector's apology that afternoon, Marley was still stung by his words. She knew she wasn't using him the way Jacleen was. Sure, he gave her a ride to Tech, but he was going there anyway. If he actually didn't see a difference between giving her a ride to class and chauffeuring Jacleen around, then fine.

She could go back to taking the bus.

She pulled out her phone and sent him a text. "Taking bus—c u 2morrow."

As soon as Tech let out, she left quickly. She wanted to be on the bus before Hector came out.

Her plan fell apart when she saw a crowd at the bus stop and realized the bus was running late. Soon the Lexus pulled up to the curb. Hector lowered the window.

"Get in," he said.

The other people at the stop looked at Marley.

"Go," she said. "I don't need a ride."

"Come on, Marls," he said. "I said I was sorry."

"Girl, you should get in that car!" a woman said. Others laughed.

"Can *I* get in that car?" a guy asked. The crowd laughed harder.

"Don't make me beg, okay?" Hector said. "Please?"

Marley shrugged and opened the door.

"Girl, make him beg!" the first woman said.

Marley waved and slammed the door.

"I'm really, really sorry," Hector said. "I've got stuff going on. But it's not you. I shouldn't have said what I said. I like riding with you over here. And I know you're not trying to use me, okay?"

Marley nodded. "I shouldn't have made fun of Jacleen," she said as an apology. "She just has a way of making me feel so, so—I don't know. She smells of Chanel, and I smell like the disgusting hotdogs at the Kwik," she said.

"So that's why I'm always hungry after I drop you off!" Hector said with a laugh. "Makes you feel any better, I kinda like those hotdogs!"

Marley laughed.

"Hey," Hector said, putting his hand on her arm. Marley turned toward him with a questioning look. "Friends again?" he asked.

Not for the first time, Marley thought about how good he looked. Maybe other girls wouldn't think so, but she did. She knew it was at least partly because she knew him so well. And she knew the reason she made sarcastic comments about Jacleen was because of how she felt about Hector.

"Always," she said, settling back against the lush seat. She would never give away how she felt about him—never. To him, she was his buddy, commiserating about trying to balance life at two schools. Beyond that, nothing.

"Hey, how are you coming with that History Day project for Mister Kerwin?" Hector asked. "Who are you working with?"

"Joss White and Eva Morales," Marley said, naming two high school classmates. "But we're having trouble getting together. Between going to Tech and working, I don't have the free time that they have," she added.

History Day was a big event at Cap Central. Teams of students put together reports, exhibits, performances, or documentaries of events they felt had changed history. It was a competition, with the winner continuing on to the regional contest. Joss and Eva were fun girls who Marley enjoyed hanging with. She was glad when they were grouped together.

"Do you work at the Kwik all weekend?" Hector asked.

"I'm supposed to," Marley answered. "But I was actually going to see if I could have one of those days off. The three of us are supposed to get together to work on our project. Who are you working with?" she asked.

"Actually, Carlos and Ferg," he said with a laugh. Carlos Garcia and Lionel "Ferg" Ferguson were Joss and Eva's boyfriends. "We're supposed to get together this weekend too, but I work Saturdays at the garage."

He pulled up in front of the Kwik n'Carry. Marley gathered her things and opened the door.

"Well, thanks, as always," she said.

"Anytime," he said. "Truly." He smiled at her, and Marley felt herself get warm inside.

"Okay," Marley said with a laugh. She was glad they had made up. She knew there was never a chance for any other kind of a relationship with him because of Jacleen. But she was glad to have him as one of her closest friends.

After her shift ended, Marley took the bus home. She went inside her apartment and found total chaos. The twins were crying. There was a box of oat-ring cereal spilled on the kitchen floor. And her four-year-old sister wasn't wearing any pants.

"Mama?" Marley called out. "What's going on? Why is everyone still up?" She threw her backpack on the floor and picked up the twin who was crying the hardest. She kissed him on the nose and continued to hold him while she looked for the broom to clean up the mess.

"Oh, hi, baby," her mother said.

"You okay?" Marley asked, setting the baby down on the couch.

"Yeah. Been a long day, that's all," her mother said. "Now that the cable is gone, there's

not so much for them to do. Seems like someone's been wailing all day."

In an effort to cut their budget, Marley's
mother had given up everything that wasn't
essential. Cable was one of the last so-called
luxuries to go. Without it, they couldn't watch
any TV.

Losing the cable meant no Internet connec-
tion either. But they had sold their computer
many months back, so it didn't much matter.
Marley had to use the computers at Cap Central
to work on her Tech homework.

"Let's get them washed up and put them in
bed," Marley said. "I'll help."

She picked up both twins and carried them
into the bathroom. She turned the water on in
the sink and waited for it to get warm. A few
minutes later, it was still cold.

"Mom? Do you know why there's no hot
water?" she called out.

"Probably because to have hot water, you
have to pay the gas bill," her mother said bitterly.
"Get used to it."

Marley took a washcloth and scrubbed all of
the babies. Then she got them into fresh diapers

and their pj's. She settled them into their crib, then she got her four-year-old sister into bed. Finally, she joined her mother in the kitchen.

She opened the refrigerator door. There was nothing inside. She closed it again and took a box of macaroni and cheese out of the cupboard. The box had come from a food pantry. Marley was grateful that people donated so much to the pantries.

Not for the first time, she vowed that when she had enough money to spare, she would donate food every chance she got. She measured out the water into a pan and turned on the stove.

"Honey, I hate to ask, but when's the next time you get paid?" her mother asked.

Marley looked at the wall calendar. "Every other Friday. So two days from now," she said. "Why?"

Her mother shook her head. "I'm a little worried about the rent," she said. "Any idea how much your check will be?"

"About the same as always," Marley said. "Which isn't enough for the whole rent. Can you talk to Mister Deane about letting us pay half and then half again in two weeks?"

"I can try," her mother said. "I don't know how long he's going to let us go, though," she said. "He told me last time that he wouldn't allow us to do that again."

"I could talk to Mister Vimal at the store about working more hours," Marley said.

"Could you do it soon?" her mother asked. "We could really use the cash. You're working both days this upcoming weekend, right? What about tomorrow night and Friday?"

Marley's heart fell. Mr. Vimal needed her Saturday. But he had agreed to let her take Sunday off. She really wanted to hang out with her friends. She also knew her family needed the money she made.

Marley tried not to feel resentful. But sometimes she just wanted to be able to hang out without worrying that her family would go hungry if she did.

"I'm scheduled for tomorrow night, Friday, and Saturday," she said. "I guess I'll talk to him about Sunday."

The water boiled and Marley dumped in the macaroni.

"As long as it's days," her mother said. "I

worry about you working there after dark."

"If I work more hours, some of them are going to be after dark," Marley said. "But don't worry. There's a silent alarm behind the counter. And I wouldn't fight anyone who tries to rob us. We've been told we would actually get fired if we resist a robbery. How's that for a crazy policy?" she added with a laugh.

Her mother didn't even smile. "I just feel so bad about all this," she said. "I keep looking for a job, but it's so hard. I took the kids to the library today, but it was tough to control them during the hour I had on the computer there."

"You know, I'm on computers all day at Cap Central and Tech," Marley said. She drained the macaroni and mixed in the orange cheese packet. "I'll take your résumé and all your information and apply as if I'm you. What do you think about that?"

She took out two forks and handed one to her mother. She put the pot in the middle of the table. They both picked at the cheesy noodles.

"Worth a try, I guess," her mother said. "I just hope I can find someone to watch the kids if I ever do get a job. Well, you probably have homework," she added, standing up. "I'll clean up. And, Marley, thanks. I don't know what I'd do without you."

Marley kissed her mother's cheek. "Something's going to work out," she said. "I just know it."

Marley went into the room she shared with her little sister. In the darkness away from her mother's worried face, she sat on the bed and put her head in her hands. She needed to help her family find money—and fast.

CHAPTER 5

HECTOR

Looking back on it, Hector was embarrassed at how gullible he had been. On his first day at the garage, Dez Arnold explained what he expected Hector to do. Every Saturday, he was to sweep out the bays, clean the bathroom, straighten the supplies, and be available for whatever Dez or the mechanics needed help with. He had introduced him to Maxim Dudich and Sergio Batiste, the two mechanics. Neither man was particularly friendly. Hector decided he would avoid both of them.

Dez showed him the office, the two bays, and the restroom. To the left of the office was a door with a shiny deadbolt lock on it. Hector had wondered where it led. He didn't ask. Dez never said. Hector tried to forget about it.

All that first day, Hector was aware of sounds coming from another part of the building. The mechanics wouldn't often be in the bays, but he could hear work continuing. He suspected there was another level where other people were working.

At the end of the day, Dez threw him a set of keys. "Here are the keys to the Lexus. You can keep it as long as you're working for me. Just be careful with it. Don't get pulled over—not for anything. Hear me?"

Hector felt himself grinning. "I hear you!" he said happily.

He carefully drove the car home, staying well within the speed limits. When he pulled up in front of his house, he opened the glove compartment to see if the registration and insurance cards were inside. He found a registration card in the name of Harold McAlpin. He wondered who that was, and why the guy let Dez Arnold— and now Hector—drive his car.

A week later, he understood.

Hector had arrived at the garage around eight thirty. He swept out the bays, but they didn't look like they had seen much use. As always, the two cars were out in front with their hoods up.

He moved on to cleaning the restroom, but he realized they were out of paper towels. He started to enter Dez's office to ask him what he should do.

"You should have thought of that before you borrowed my money," Dez was saying. "You knew the score."

Hector didn't want to hear the conversation, but he had already opened the office door. A man was sitting across from Dez. He had a miserable look on his face.

"Sorry!" Hector said. "I'll come back."

"No, that's okay," Dez said. "I need you to do something for me."

He turned to the man. "Hand them over," he said.

The man hesitated.

"Now!" Dez barked.

"Please!" the man pleaded.

Dez waited a minute, and then opened a desk drawer. He pulled out a handgun. He didn't point it at the man or do anything threatening.

But just seeing the gun made the man put up his hands.

Hector nearly gasped. He felt like he was frozen in place.

"Dez, no, man!" the man said. "I'll pay, I swear! Just give me a few more days. I'll get you the money. On my children's lives, I swear I will!"

It sounded like the man was crying.

"You've got a week," Dez said coldly. He was still holding the gun. "Next Saturday if I don't have the ten grand you owe me? It's out of here. Now, put them on the desk and get lost. You make me sick."

The man put the keys on the desk and walked out, his shoulders hunched over.

Dez put the gun away. "You gonna work here, you gonna see stuff like that from time to time," he said. "I help people low on cash. Sometimes they get in over their heads. My price is always their wheels. They know what they're getting into ahead of time, but they do it anyway. You okay with that?"

Hector wasn't sure what Dez was asking him. But it seemed clear: the guy had to pay back a loan using money or his car. He nodded. He

was still so shocked that he didn't trust himself
to speak.

"You may see stuff here that don't look
exactly right," Dez said. "You gonna be cool with
that no matter what you see?"

Hector couldn't imagine what the older man
was referring to.

"Yeah, we're cool," he said.

"Good, man," Dez said. He tossed the keys
to Hector. "These are for the Beemer out front.
Drive it around back and wait in front of the
doors. Honk twice. When the doors open, drive
it in."

Hector went out front. Parked in front of
the shop was a beautiful white BMW 320i. He
started the car and admired how it purred.

He drove around back. Across the driveway was a high fence with a sliding gate that
was open. The ground sloped down to a base-
ment floor below the street level that faced MLK
Avenue. He wasn't surprised to see two more
bay doors. It explained why the building looked
so large. He honked. Soon the bay door opened.
Maxim waved him in. Hector got out and looked
around. Behind him, Sergio closed the bay.

The place was filled with sections of car bodies lying in pieces. Hector could see the partial remains of at least two cars in different parts of the large room. Two men were working on dismantling them.

"Keys?" Maxim asked, holding out his hand.

Hector handed him the keys. He continued to look around.

"Get back upstairs," Maxim said gruffly. "This way." He led Hector to a door in the corner and opened it. Hector went up the stairs and came out of the door by Dez's office.

Dez saw him and called him in. "So what did you see down there?" he asked.

Hector was confused. Surely Dez knew what was going on in his own shop.

"Just some guys working on cars," he said. "Are those the cars of people who couldn't pay their loans?"

Dez was quiet for a moment. "Pretty much," he said.

"So you use their cars for parts for the cars you work on up here?" Hector asked.

Again Dez hesitated before answering. "Yeah, or I sell them to other garages who need them."

"Makes sense," Hector said, nodding.

"Meanwhile, I got another job for you," Dez said. He handed Hector another set of keys. "There's a Jeep Cherokee out front. I need you to drive it to this address and leave it with the keys inside."

He wrote an address on the back of an invoice sheet.

Hector picked up the invoice. "Nineteen hundred Massachusetts Avenue," he said, reading the address. "The old D.C. General Hospital? Who do I give it to?" Hector asked.

"No one. D.C. General is now a homeless shelter. You leave it and walk away."

"But someone's gonna steal it!" Hector said incredulously. "It won't last five minutes." It didn't make sense to him.

"Look, here's how it works," Dez said. "Some folks can't pay their loans. So I pick up their cars and sell them. Others are worth more in insurance money if they get stolen. This is one of those."

"So you *want* it to get stolen?" Hector asked in disbelief.

"Pretty much," Dez answered. "Guy who

owes me money hasn't paid. He's got an insured car. Car gets stolen, insurance pays him, he pays me. Everybody's happy."

Except the insurance company, Hector thought. He reached for the keys and took the paper with the address on it.

That had been a few months ago. Since then, Hector had lost count of how many cars he'd left in the worst parts of D.C. The process was always the same: Dez Arnold would write an address on the back of one of his invoices, describing where Hector should leave a car. It was always a different place. But always in a part of D.C. where a car with the key in the ignition wouldn't last five minutes.

Hector figured that what he was doing was not technically illegal. He wasn't stealing the cars, and he wasn't getting the insurance money.

Technically was one thing. Morally was another.

He knew it was wrong.

He could quit at any time. But that would mean giving up the Lexus.

He hated being the guy who added to people's misery just for the sake of a hot car.

But he had to face facts.

Apparently, that's exactly who he was.

CHAPTER 6

MARLEY

On Thursday morning Marley kissed her mother goodbye and left the apartment. She walked down the two flights of stairs to Oates Street. Heading toward Cap Central High, she walked past apartment buildings and row houses.

Now that the neighborhood was becoming trendy, some of the row houses had been renovated and expanded upward. The "pop-ups," as they were called, looked out of proportion to their shorter neighbors.

But Marley's dislike of the architecture was not the main thing she thought about when she saw money flowing in. The hipper the neighborhood got, the more people might be willing to pay for rent. And it would take a saint to allow the Macomb family to keep missing their rent payments when others were anxious to move in.

She went to the school cafeteria to eat breakfast. There she ran into Eva and Joss. She set her tray down on the table beside them.

"I'm so glad you're here!" Joss said. "You're coming over Saturday night to work on the project, aren't you?"

"I can't," Marley said. "I have to work. Can we get together Sunday instead?"

"Well, I guess so, but that sucks," Eva complained. "We never get to see you anymore now that you're not here in the afternoons. How's Tech going anyway?"

"It's good," Marley answered. "I like it, but it's a pain getting there and back. Good thing Hector Turcio goes too. I ride with him."

"Hmm. I'm surprised that the lovely Jacleen allows him to let you in his car," Joss said. "She's got him on a very short leash."

Marley rolled her eyes. "True that," she said. "She looks like she'd like to shoot me whenever she sees me in his car. Maybe she thinks my ugly will leave a mark."

"Ugly? Girl, you trippin'!" Eva said. "More

likely she knows the more time Hector spends with you, the greater the risk he'll realize there's nothing to her besides a pretty face."

"You really think Jacleen is capable of thinking that through?" Joss said nastily. "You're giving her more credit than she deserves!"

"C'mon," Marley said. "Give her a break. She can't help being pretty."

"I'm not really blaming her," Joss said. "It's Hector who's being stupid. I mean, really, does he think she's sticking around because he's drop-dead gorgeous?"

"But he is, sort of, don't you think?" Marley said. "I mean, those eyes!"

"Well, well, *well*," Eva said with a smile. "So that's how it is, eh?

"Nah," Marley lied. "We're just really good friends."

"I bet more than one couple has gotten together from being stuck in D.C. traffic!" Joss said.

"Not going to happen!" Marley said. "Trust me! He has eyes only for two things: that car and Jacleen. And we truly are good friends. I'd hate to mess that up."

"He just needs to notice you, that's all," Eva said. "But he's blinded by the Jacleen light. Now if we could just get her out of the way ..." She looked around the cafeteria. "Now who could we stick her with?"

"Hey, ladies, you looking fine this morning!" Luther Ransome said, setting his tray on the table and taking the seat beside Marley.

"Girls, I think we have a winner!" Joss said, her voice brimming with laughter. Luther was a star athlete and favorite bad boy with girls who liked that type. His reputation had suffered a bit recently when he was suspected of hacking into the school's computers to change his grades. As a result, he was kicked off the basketball team. Without sports to bolster his reputation, fewer girls were hanging around him.

"Which one of you wants to walk with me to class?" Luther said, oblivious to the girls' amusement. "I'm feeling mighty lonely."

Just then, Jacleen Thompson carried her tray over to the trash cans.

"There's Jacleen," Eva said. "She's by herself. You'd look good together," she added.

"Girl, you speaking the truth," Luther

declared, standing up. "Ladies, it's been—whatever," he said, walking toward Jacleen.

"Well, we tried!" Joss said, still laughing. The three girls stood up and got rid of their trays.

"See you Sunday, okay?" Eva said.

Marley waved and went to English.

After her classes, she gathered up her things and waited by Hector's car when it was time to go to Tech. She was quiet on the trip. She kept trying to come up with ways to pay the rent. She wondered what would happen if they missed a month.

She knew there were homeless shelters in D.C. for families who had lost their homes. She couldn't imagine what life in a shelter would be like. Some places, she knew, had rooms for families, while others were just one big room housing many families. They both sounded awful, but better than living on the street or in their car.

"What's up with you, Marls?" Hector finally asked. "Not like you to be so quiet."

"Sorry," Marley answered. "A lot on my mind, I guess."

"Want to talk about it?" Hector asked.

Marley didn't want to tell him about her family's problems. She was embarrassed at the thought. She didn't want anyone to know how poor they were.

"Just family stuff," she said.

"Twins staying out late, getting drunk, boosting cars?" he teased.

"Something like that," she giggled. "Well ... not exactly since they're only a year old. Actually, you're not even close."

"Any way I can help?" he asked.

"Not really," she mumbled. "But thanks."

Out of the corner of her eye, she saw Hector looking at her. She turned toward him.

"What?" she asked.

"Nothing," he said. "You know you can trust me, right?" He pulled into a parking spot.

Marley *did* know. But her family's problems were not something she felt like sharing. She put her hand on his arm. "I do trust you," she said. "I just—" She shook her head. "I'm just not ready to talk about it."

After class, Hector dropped Marley off at the Kwik n'Carry.

The store was busy. It wasn't until Marley was about to leave that she had an opportunity to ask Mr. Vimal if she could work more hours.

"Unfortunately, D.C. is strict about limiting kids' hours. There's not much I can do," he said. "But I've only been scheduling you till seven or eight at night. I can schedule you till ten if you'd like. You could start tomorrow night."

Marley didn't feel like she had much choice.

"I'll do it," she said.

"There is one other option," he added hesitantly.

Marley looked at him quizzically.

"If you were available, you could work the day shift. I really need someone. Five days a week, eight hours a day. Full time, so you'd get benefits."

"But I have school!" Marley said, confused.

"Right. But keep it in mind. If you really need the money, you might think about working for a while. Instead of school."

"You mean dropping out?" Marley answered, horrified. She had never even considered dropping out of school.

"I am just saying to think about it," Mr.

Vimal said. "Meanwhile, you can stay until ten tomorrow and Saturday, and I'll put you back on the schedule for Sunday. Sound good?"

Marley nodded. She'd have to tell Eva and Joss she couldn't get together on Sunday.

Drop out of school. She even hated the words. It might be the answer to her family's problems.

But it would be the end of her dreams.

CHAPTER 7

HECTOR

Hector woke up in a bad mood. He'd run so many errands for his family and Jacleen the night before that he hadn't even had a chance to eat dinner until around nine thirty. He felt like he was driving the world's most expensive taxicab.

His mother had a list of errands he needed to do for her: go to the grocery store, pick up his younger brother, and pick up his grandmother from the dialysis clinic three times a week.

He was also disgusted about the emptiness of his so-called relationship with Jacleen.

He knew the "relationship" wasn't going anywhere. Truth was, he knew it wasn't even a relationship. They rarely did anything together. They spent time together, sure, since she always seemed to have somewhere she needed him to take her.

He'd driven her numerous times to get her nails and hair done, to her friends' houses, and to shopping areas across the line in Maryland. Every once in a while she'd press against him and let him kiss her. Quickly.

But spend an evening together? Never.

Last night, he asked her if she wanted to hang out Friday night, maybe see a movie or get something to eat. As always, she gave some lame excuse for why she had to be with her friends. It almost didn't matter. They had little to talk about beyond gossip about their classmates.

Jacleen hung out with Brennay Baxter and Zakia Johnson, two popular girls known to be mean. The only topic Jacleen got really animated about was herself. Hector couldn't help but compare his conversations with Jacleen to those he had with Marley.

He and Marley never ran out of things to talk about. She was never mean. And when they weren't talking, it was perfectly comfortable. When he and Jacleen weren't talking, he felt pressure to find something to fill the silence.

But there was no denying that Jacleen looked good. Very good. He liked the looks he got when they were together, especially when they were in his car. He felt like every guy he saw wished he were Hector Turcio. Wanted to be the guy with a girlfriend who looked like Jacleen. Who had the money for a car like the Lexus.

The real Hector Turcio knew it was all fake.

And then there was the garage. He knew he was walking a very thin line that separated the legal from the criminal. Dez Arnold let him tinker with the cars out front or when someone brought in a car for a minor repair.

Hector had gotten very good at changing the oil, topping off other fluids, tightening bolts, rotating tires, and other work. But he didn't really have a chance to help with more major repairs: transmission work, timing belts, water pumps, or other big items.

No one seemed to bring their cars in for this kind of work. Because Dez Arnold wasn't actually a mechanic.

He was a loan shark.

He was getting very rich by loaning money to people he knew couldn't pay it back. His operation was a huge insurance scam, aided by the desperate people who would do whatever they needed to get money fast. Hector had lost count of the number of cars he had abandoned for Dez. Or the number of desperate "customers" he saw turning over their keys.

And then there was the work in the back of the shop. Hector knew Dez was running a chop shop: cutting up cars to sell them for parts. He suspected many of the cars had been stolen.

That afternoon, Hector had been so wrapped up in his own problems, he hadn't noticed how quiet Marley was until they were almost to Tech. He was used to the easy conversation they always shared, but lately she seemed to be preoccupied.

He gave himself a little mental shake and turned to her. "So what do you have going on this weekend?" he asked.

"Work, work, and more work," she said. There was a bitter tone to her voice that he hadn't heard before.

"You like your job that much?" he tried to joke. Marley just turned to look out the window.

"Not even a little," she said. "And I told my boss I'd work the late shift tonight and tomorrow night. I really don't want to do it, but I feel like I have no choice."

"Why not?" Hector asked.

"Because we need the money," Marley said.

Hector wasn't surprised. He had suspected that her family was struggling. But he really didn't know what to say. She had never opened up about her family before.

"Your mom doing okay?" he asked.

"As okay as someone can do who has three kids under the age of four and no job," she said bitterly. "Not her fault, but still ..." her voice trailed off.

"That's tough," he said.

"Yeah, well, that's life," she said. "How about you? You seeing the princess this weekend?"

Hector decided to let her comment pass. "Nah," he said. "She had a few other things planned for this weekend."

"You're too good for her. You know that, right?" Marley said.

Hector looked at her and smiled. "Thanks, Mom," he joked.

"How are things going over at the garage?" Marley asked.

Hector shook his head slightly. "Promise not to gloat?" he asked.

Marley shook her head. "I won't," she said seriously.

"It's not what I expected," Hector said. "The guy is running a loan operation. He lends money to people who use their cars as security. Most end up not paying it back."

Hector didn't know why he had confessed this to Marley. He knew she didn't approve of his choices. But her honesty about her family's struggles made him feel like he could trust her to hear him out without judging him. And actually, it felt good to finally tell someone.

"Wow. That's cold," Marley said. "So what happens then?

"They turn the car over to him at the garage. Or sometimes we leave the car somewhere to be stolen. Insurance pays the customer, who pays Dez back what he's owed."

"What happens if they don't give the money back to him?" Marley asked. "What does he do to them?"

"Hasn't happened yet that I know of," Hector said. "Probably not anything good."

"Bound to some day," Marley said. "So what's your role in this little scam?"

Hector shot her a look. He didn't like the tone in her voice. "I drive the cars and leave them," Hector said.

"You know you have to quit, right?" Marley said. "This isn't going to end well. For the poor people who are scamming their insurance companies. For Dez Arnold, not that I care about that scumbag. Or for you. You're the only one I care about."

"You care about me?" Hector said with the hint of a smile. "Well, that just made my day!"

"I'm serious," Marley said. "How long do you think it's going to be before someone doesn't play by Dez's rules and he takes it to another level? He's not a guy to get his hands dirty. I'll bet you anything he'll expect you to do his dirty work. You need to get out of there. Fast."

"You know that would mean giving back this car, right?" Hector said.

"You're putting your future—your life—in danger because of a car?" Marley asked incredulously. "Listen to yourself! Don't have a car? Take the bus like the rest of us do!"

"But my grandmother needs to get to dialysis. And my mom needs me to—"

"Hector." Marley put her hand on his arm. "Look at me."

Hector looked. He could see the concern in her eyes. He had never noticed before how unusual her eyes were. They were light brown with flecks of gold in them. He wondered why he hadn't really looked at her before this. She wasn't what some people might think of as pretty. But there was something about her that was beautiful to him.

He realized she was expecting him to say something. "What?" he asked. His voice came out sounding a little funny. "What?" he repeated.

"You can work all of that out. They managed before you had a car, and they can again. Give the car back, and get out while you can," Marley said firmly but kindly. "And promise me you won't do anything that crosses the line between what you're doing now and what Dez Arnold is inevitably going to ask you to do."

" 'Cause you care about me, right?" Hector said, trying to lighten the mood. He parked the car in Tech's lot.

"Nah," Marley said, getting out of the car. "I was just playin'."

Hector only half-listened to Mr. Woodbine that afternoon. As the class worked on timing belts, he thought about Marley's words. He knew it was probably true. There would come a time when Dez Arnold asked him to do something that would take his involvement to another level. He hoped he would have the courage to say no.

When class was about over, he took off his jumpsuit and started to leave.

"Class, get back in your seats," Mr. Woodbine barked.

Everyone groaned as they returned to their desks.

"I am very, very unhappy!" the teacher said. "You are not going home until you hear a little lecture about responsibility."

He sat on the edge of his desk. "A few years ago, I was teaching this class and I let a student use a set of my personal tools. I had etched WW and my phone number on each one in the foolish, naïve hope that doing so would protect them

from theft. Back in those days, I was not as dili-
gent as I am now about making students return
all tools to their proper place."

He looked around the classroom, making
eye contact with his students. "Then I came in
one morning and found the place ransacked. The
most expensive tools were all gone, as well as my
own personal set. The police could do nothing.
Nothing! Thousands of dollars' worth of tools
lost. I vowed that day I would never lock up at
the end of the day without being able to account
for every tool. A place for everything and everything in its place," he said. "Look around at the
mess you left. Is everything in its place?"

The room was disorganized with tools left
out. The class grumbled.

"So get to work."

CHAPTER 8

MARLEY

Hector was so late coming out of class that Marley thought about taking the bus. But on a Friday at that time of day, traffic was a nightmare. She called Mr. Vimal and told him she would get there when she could.

She wasn't looking forward to working later. For one thing, she was tired and would have liked to relax. Or hang with her friends.

But to be honest with herself, she knew what the real problem was.

She was scared.

But Hector arrived, and she was not late for her job.

The Kwik n'Carry was on Benning Road, a major thoroughfare in Northeast. But after dark, there wasn't much foot traffic on the section where the store was located. She didn't relish the thought of working then, even though she would be working with Emmitt Drysdale, an older guy who'd been there for years.

She knew there were security cameras inside and outside the store. Mr. Vimal even had a baseball bat behind the counter. The store was robbed at least once a year. Mr. Vimal told her that if anyone demanded money, she should just give him whatever he asked for. Marley knew she wouldn't relax until her shift ended.

The store was busy early in the evening. Around nine, Emmitt went outside to smoke a cigarette. While he was gone, a guy walked in who looked suspicious. Marley watched him as he walked around the store. She thought he might be shoplifting but didn't confront him. He finally came up to the counter.

She braced herself for what might happen next. He put a package of diapers on the counter, along with some baby wipes and a roll of toilet paper. Then he dumped a pile of candy on the counter.

"Emergency supplies," he said with a smile.

Marley laughed and relaxed. "Who gets the candy?" she asked.

"I do. After I get those kids down for the night!" he joked, shaking his head. He pulled out a twenty and then stuffed the change Marley gave him into the container for donations to the Special Olympics.

The door opened and a nicely dressed man walked in. He went over to the drinks cooler. Marley looked at her watch. Only fifteen more minutes to go. Mr. Vimal had given her some boxes of candy to put out. She used a box cutter to open them and came around the counter to fill up the bins.

She saw the man walking toward the counter and assumed he was about to pay. Just then, the door to the store opened. Emmitt walked back in.

"How you doing?" he said to the customer coming around the counter. "You need help, Marley?"

"I can get it. Thanks!" Marley said as she stocked the candy.

The man looked from Marley to Emmitt and

back again. He pulled out his wallet and paid for his beverage. Then he left the store.

At ten, the door opened and Marley's replacement came in. Marley grabbed her sweatshirt and said good night. She walked to the bus stop on Benning Road. Between waiting for the bus and walking home from her stop, she didn't get home until after eleven.

She hated this. She didn't want to work on Saturday night too. She wanted to quit. She wanted to have a normal, carefree time in high school, like her classmates had. But she knew she had no choice. Her family needed her.

CHAPTER 9

HECTOR

Hector was about to leave for the garage Saturday morning when Jacleen called. She said she needed him to drive her to the photography studio so she could get her new headshots. Even though it would mean getting to the garage late, Hector picked her up.

The photography studio turned out to be in Northwest, not terribly far from their neighborhood. Even on a Saturday morning traffic was terrible, as it seemed to be all the time lately. Now that trendy restaurants and stores had begun springing up in the area, there were cars parked everywhere. Lots of people cruised around looking for spaces.

Being stuck in traffic gave them a chance

to talk. Rather, Jacleen talked, not seeming to notice that he had little to say. She told him of her plans for the weekend. How she expected to look in her new photos. The new shoes she needed in just the right color. How she was going to help her friend Brennay Baxter with her hair. And on and on. Hector's mind wandered while she talked.

"I might have to give back this car," he blurted out when she took a breath.

"What?" she nearly shrieked. "What are you talking about? I thought this was your car!"

"It's borrowed," he said. He knew he was running the risk of losing her by saying it. But he almost didn't care. And it would be a true test of how she felt about him. Whether she would want to see him even if he didn't have the car, or if the car was his most attractive feature.

"Why would you have to give it back?" she asked.

"Because I don't like the guy who lent it to me, and I don't really want to deal with him anymore," he explained.

"So what?" she said, her voice rising to a screech. "Car like this? I'd do anything to have it! I wouldn't care what it was. You don't give back a car like this!"

"What if what you had to do to borrow it is illegal?"

"Don't matter. You keep the car," she said. He could hear the anger in her voice.

"Doesn't," he said softly. "Doesn't matter."

"What?" she said. "I can't hear you."

"Nothing," he said.

"So are we still together or what?" she asked.

"Together? We don't see each other that much," Hector said. He didn't know why he was all of a sudden being honest. "I wasn't sure we were together, actually."

"What I mean is, you gonna keep this car?"

Hector looked at her sharply. "Is that your definition of us being together?" he asked. "If I have a car, we're together. If I don't, we aren't?"

Jacleen was quiet for a moment. "Keep the car," she said coldly. "I mean it."

Hector knew he should end things right then. But he couldn't bring himself to say the words.

"So then if we're *together*, you want to get together tonight?" he asked, knowing the answer.

"Go dancing at Club?" Club was an under-21 dance club not far from Cap Central.

"I'm busy," Jacleen said.

"Of course you are," Hector said sarcastically.

"What's that mean?" she said.

"I was being sarcastic," Hector explained.

"Well, quit being spastic," she said. "And pick me up in an hour."

Hector almost laughed. Instead he said, "I can't. I have to work at the garage. You're going to have to find another way home."

"Like how?" Jacleen asked. "You should have told me that before you said you wanted to drive me here!"

Hector never told her he wanted to drive her any place. But he didn't bother to correct her.

"You're right near Metro Center," he said, naming one of the main transfer stations for the D.C. subway. "Take the Red Line to the NoMa/Gallaudet station."

"And then what?" Jacleen said. "How do I get home from there?"

"You could try walking," Hector said. "It's not that far."

"Do you have any idea how long it took me

to get my hair this straight?" she said. "This humidity? I'll be a mess!"

Hector found her complaints exhausting. "I don't know, Jac," he said. "I have to get going. Call somebody else for a ride. Take a cab. Whatever."

Jacleen got out of the car and slammed the door angrily. Then she knocked at the window.

Hector rolled it down. He hoped she was going to thank him for the ride.

"Don't ever call me Jac," she said.

Hector rolled his eyes in exasperation. He put the window back up and headed toward the garage. Driving from Northwest to Southeast took forever. He finally got to the garage around eleven. He didn't see Dez Arnold when he arrived, but Maxim told him to test the radiator on the Lincoln out front to see if there was a leak.

Hector grabbed a wrench from a tool bench in the corner and opened the hood of the Lincoln. He realized the wrench was the wrong size. When he went to put it back, something caught his eye. He looked closer. Etched in the metal beside the manufacturer's name were the initials WW.

He knew right away what he was holding:

one of Mr. Woodbine's stolen tools. He remembered Dez had once told him that he'd had Mr. Woodbine when he was at Tech. He shook his head in disgust. He put the wrench in his pocket and picked up the right one. He got to work on the car. His spirits lifted a bit. He really enjoyed working on cars.

His good mood didn't last long. Dez Arnold came in around noon. He watched Hector for a while, making a few suggestions. Then he said, "Take a break, Hector. I want to talk to you about a job."

Hector put down his wrench and followed Dez into the office. "Have a seat," Dez said, motioning to one of his extra chairs.

Hector was suspicious. Dez never talked to him this way. He wondered what he would ask him to do.

"So how you like the Lexus?" Dez said.

Hector was surprised. That wasn't what he thought Dez was going to say.

"I like it fine," he said. "It's a great car. That V-6 engine gets—"

"It is a great car," Dez agreed, cutting him off. "How would you like to buy it from me?"

"Wish I could!" Hector said with a laugh. "Too bad I don't have the cash."

"Maybe you could buy it without actually having to come up with the cash," Dez said.

"How would I do that?" Hector asked.

"Odd jobs here and there," Dez said noncommittally. "Let's come up with a price, shall we? Let's see. The car's a couple of years old, but it's cherry. Let me check the Blue Book value on it."

He hit a few keys on his computer. Hector already knew what the car was worth. He had looked it up himself, hoping he could make Dez an offer for it. But he didn't have that kind of money. Heck, he knew he'd probably never have enough money to spend that much on a car.

"Hmm," Dez said. He named a price. It was much higher than what Hector knew the car was selling for around town.

"I actually looked it up," Hector said. "You sure you looking at the right model? Because this one's current value is less than that."

"Let's see," Dez said, hitting more keys. "Oh, you're right, I was looking at the wrong car."

Hector knew he was lying, but he let it go.

"So here's the thing," Dez said. "I got some

stuff needs done. A little more risky than what you were doing before. I got a lot of customers behind on their payments. But they're not coming in to drop off their cars. They knew the score, and they been avoiding my calls. Time to get tougher. You in?"

Hector didn't like the sound of this. "What would I have to do?" he asked.

"Thing is, before I lend money, I ask for a set of keys," Dez said. "Just in case. Usually, just knowing I got the keys is enough to keep people paying. Hear me?"

Hector nodded.

"So I got the keys. And I know where the cars are. I just need someone to go pick up the cars and drive them back here. Not like you're jacking the car or anything since we got the actual keys."

Hector didn't answer. He knew what Dez was suggesting was dangerous.

"Each of these jobs you do for me will earn you a grand toward the car. In exchange for doing this legwork? I'm willing to let it go for ten grand. Pick up ten cars for me, the car will be yours free and clear. You're a hard worker. I'm thinking you'll own your own wheels in three months. Maybe less. What do you say?"

Hector was torn. He knew it was wrong. There was no way to even fool himself into thinking it wasn't dangerous. But on the other hand, buying the car from Dez meant that in a couple of months, he'd own the car free and clear. He could quit the garage and get as far away from Dez and his shady operation as possible.

All of a sudden, he thought about Marley. What she would say if she knew. She'd tell him to walk away. No doubt. And she'd be right. He sighed. He just wouldn't tell her. And when he finally owned the car, he'd be able to tell her he had quit working for Dez.

"I'll do it," he said.

"Good man!" Dez said. He pulled out one of his invoices and turned it over. "Here's the address," he said. He wrote something down. He opened a locked cabinet that was full of keys. He took one out of the cabinet and handed it to Hector.

"Black Audi A4," he said. "Should be parked right out front. I'll write down the plate number for you." He wrote the number on the paper.

"Bring the car back here, and you can take off after that," he said. "I don't expect any trouble. If it happens, get yourself out of there. But keep the keys so we can try again, hear me?"

Hector was reluctant to go. He really didn't want to do this. But he really wanted to buy the car. "When do you want me to go?" he asked.

"Now," Dez said. "Guy always sleeps late. Probably won't even know it's gone till late afternoon."

Hector picked up the paper and put it in his wallet. He used his cell phone to look up how to get to the address by bus. He took one bus, transferred to another, and got off at a stop a few blocks from the address. He walked down the street once to see if anyone was looking.

He didn't see anybody, so he circled around and used the remote to open the doors. He turned the key and the car started up. He pulled away from the curb just as a front door burst open.

"Hey, what are you—" a guy yelled.

The guy continued to yell, but Hector couldn't hear him anymore. He drove back to Dez's garage and parked out front.

"Pull it around back," Dez said.

Hector got in and pulled around to the back bays, where it seemed most of the garage's work was done.

Dez came down the stairs. "Any trouble?" he asked.

"Nah," Hector said. "Guy wasn't happy, though."

"They never are," Dez said. "Not my problem. Thanks, son. One down, nine to go."

Hector didn't stick around the garage to work. He got in the Lexus and took off. Nine more cars till it was his.

CHAPTER 10

MARLEY

Marley slept in a bit Saturday morning. When she finally got up, she saw her mother sitting at the kitchen table. She was reading what looked like a letter. Her expression was one of pure fear. Marley took out a bowl and poured herself some cereal.

"Mama, what is it?" she asked.

Without a word, her mother handed her the letter. Marley started to read the legal language.

"We're getting evicted?" she asked in horror.

Her mother nodded. "I was never able to finish paying last month's rent, and now it's due again," she said miserably.

"Oh, Mama, I got paid yesterday, but it isn't nearly enough to pay all the rent," Marley said. "What are we going to do?"

"I don't know, baby," her mother said. "We're just so far behind. Your checks help—I can't tell you how much they help. But I had to put some money into getting the car fixed so I could use it to look for jobs. And then—it just never ends," she said, sounding totally dejected.

Marley hated to see the defeated look on her mother's face. "Mama, we'll find a way," she said. "Maybe if I called the landlord?"

"You can try," her mother said. "Maybe you'll have better luck than me. Beyond that, I don't know where to turn."

Marley thought for a moment. "You know, I think there are people at school who help with stuff like this," she said. "Maybe I'll see if someone there can make some calls for us. Can I take this?" she asked, holding the eviction notice.

"Take it," her mother said. "I don't know where we're going to go. There's a shelter at the old D.C. General Hospital, so I guess we could go there."

"Don't pack up just yet," Marley said harshly. "Let me see what I can find out." She opened the refrigerator and took out a carton of milk. Before pouring it on her cereal, she shook the container. Not much left. She made a face and put the carton back in the fridge. She started eating the cereal dry.

"You're doing the best you can, Mama," she said. "I love you. I'll figure something out. I'll find the money somewhere. I promise."

"You're a good girl, Marley," her mother said. "You make me proud. You working today?"

Marley nodded. "Till ten again. And my friends are getting together to work on our History Day project. If they're still hanging out when I'm done working, I may hang with them. That okay with you?"

Her mother nodded. "I hate the thought of you working so late at that store," she said. "You promise me you'll be careful."

"Promise," Marley said, kissing her mother's cheek.

The store was busy most of the day. Mr. Vimal was there until about seven, then he left to have dinner with his family. Emmitt Drysdale relieved him, reeking of cigarette smoke.

Around nine, Emmitt went outside to smoke. The door opened. Marley relaxed when she recognized the man who had bought the soda the previous night. She expected him to go over to the cooler again. Instead, he walked directly to the counter. He was holding a gun.

"Girl, you know what this is, right?" he growled. "Now get me the cash. Move!"

Marley felt like her heart had stopped beating. She put her hands up. "I'll do it," she said, her voice shaking. "Give me a minute."

She tried to open the cash register but realized it was locked. With her knee, she hit the silent alarm button that Mr. Vimal had installed under the counter.

"Open that drawer! Now!" the guy yelled.

"I ... I need to ring something up or the drawer doesn't open," Marley said. She looked around for something to scan.

The guy grabbed some breath mints and put them on the counter. "Get moving," he said.

Marley rang up the sale and the drawer popped open. She took out the dollar bills and started gathering the fives.

"Faster!" the guy said. "Give me the twenties."

Marley grabbed the stack of bills and handed them over.

"Now the tens," the guy said.

All of a sudden, the front door flew open. Two cops were standing in the doorway.

"Freeze!" the first one yelled.

Marley didn't hesitate. As she dropped to the floor, she saw the gunman turn toward the cops.

"Drop the gun!" someone yelled.

Bang, bang, bang!

Marley didn't know who the shooter was. She cowered behind the counter, her arms wrapped around her body, her face pressed against her knees. The skin on the back of her neck felt like it was crawling. She braced herself for the shots she expected to come her way.

"Miss, are you all right?" a voice said. "Miss?"

Marley looked up. One of the cops was looking over the counter.

"Miss, you can come out. You're safe," the cop said.

Marley stood up on shaky legs. The guy who had been holding a gun on her a minute before was now lying on the floor, moaning. She gasped and looked away.

"Miss, I'm Officer Bryant from the Metropolitan Police Department," the cop said. "We're going to need you to stick around until we can get a statement from you. Meanwhile, is there someone you need to call?"

"I should call the manager," Marley said, picking up the phone. She called Mr. Vimal and briefly told him what happened. He said he was on his way. Marley hung up the phone. She could hear lots of communication on the police radios. Soon more police cars began filling up the parking lot.

Marley turned away so she couldn't see the man on the floor. None of it seemed real to her. Not the fact that someone had pointed a gun at her, or the fact that the cops had gotten there so fast. But the blood she could see seemed very real.

All of a sudden, she felt faint. It was as if the reality of how much danger she had been in finally dawned on her. She sank to the floor behind the counter and began to shake.

"Miss, is there someone you could call to stay with you while we get underway here?" Officer Bryant asked. "This is going to take a while, and you look like you're in shock."

Marley thought about whom she could call.

Her mother wouldn't be able to leave the little kids. And besides, she no longer had a phone.

Hector. That's who she wanted to have with her. She picked up the phone and called him.

"Hey, girl!" he answered cheerfully. "Slow night at work?"

"I need help," Marley said, her voice shaky.

"Anything," he said seriously.

She told him briefly what happened and asked him to come to the store. Then she told the police officers that he was on his way so that he would be allowed past the crime tape strung up outside the store.

Marley sat down behind the counter so she wouldn't have to look at the body. Only then did she notice all the money from the cash drawer that had fallen when the cops burst in. There was money everywhere.

One word popped into her head.

Rent.

She could hear Emmitt talking to the cops at the front of the store. He couldn't see her behind the counter. She looked up at the security camera. It was focused on the customer side of the counter. If she moved a certain way, she could block the camera with her body. She could pick up some bills and no one would ever know.

She looked around and saw how easy it would be to do. She reached toward the closest five and then stopped.

She knew if she stole the money, she'd be no better than the lowlife lying on the floor. And she knew she would never be able to live with herself. She put down her hand and leaned back.

Soon she heard Hector talking to the cops.

"She's over here," Officer Bryant said.

Hector came around the counter. He sat down beside her and wrapped his arms around her.

Marley began to cry. Huge, wracking sobs that made her nearly gag. Hector didn't say anything, just stroked her back and held her tight. Finally, her sobs tapered off. Hector pulled away and looked into her eyes.

"I don't suppose you have a Kleenex," he said with a smile.

"And now I look so awful!" Marley wailed, sobbing again as she buried her face against his shirt.

Hector put his hands on either side of her

face. "You look fine," he said. "I guess I don't need to ask how you're doing, though."

"It was just so scary," Marley said. "The guy looked okay, but he had a gun, and then they shot him. There's blood everywhere, and I was so scared, and—"

Hector kissed her on the forehead. "Shhh," he said. "Don't talk for a while. Just try to catch your breath."

Marley went on sitting close to him. Truth was, she didn't want him to let her go. It felt great to have his arms around her.

"You smell good," she said finally, sitting back.

"I probably smell like sweat!" Hector said with a laugh. "I was shooting hoops with Carlos and Ferg at the Trinidad Recreation Center. I'm just glad I heard the phone."

"I thought you guys were going to work on history," Marley said.

"We were, but first we played some ball. Then you called, sparing me having to do school-work on a Saturday night!"

"Miss, we need your statement now, if you can give it to us," Officer Bryant said.

Marley nodded. "Can he stay with me?" she asked, nodding toward Hector.

"Sure," the officer said. "Is there any place we can sit so I can take notes?"

"There's an office," Marley said. She stood up and brushed off her jeans. She grabbed the key and opened the door. Hector took the chair beside where she was sitting. He draped his arm across the back of his chair so he was lightly touching Marley's shoulder. Marley felt safe with him sitting there.

The officer took out a notebook and asked her to tell what she had seen. Marley told the story, starting with the man coming in the night before and ending with the shots. As she talked, she got more and more agitated. Hector took her hand in his. He laced his fingers through hers and held tight.

There was a knock at the door, and Mr. Vimal came in. He was very upset, and kept apologizing to Marley for having allowed her to work after dark. He asked what happened, and she had to go through the story again.

Finally, Hector stood up. "I'm taking her home," he said. "If you have more questions, you have her cell phone. But she's been here long enough. Okay?"

"That's fine," Officer Bryant said. "We may need more from you, Ms. Macomb, but if we do, we'll get in touch."

"Take tomorrow off, Marley, with pay," Mr. Vimal said. He stood up as well. "Officer, my money is all over the store," he said as he walked out of the office. "May I pick it up?"

Marley didn't hear the answer. She grabbed her purse from the hook in the office and shut the door.

"Can you drive me home?" she asked Hector.

"Let's go," he said.

They walked out of the store and into the cool night. The parking lot was lit by the red and blue police car lights. Crime scene tape blocked off the parking lot.

"Where did you have to park?" Marley asked.

"Not far," Hector said. He put his arm around her and pulled her close.

They got to the Lexus, and he opened the door for her. Then he went around to get in. He drove to Marley's apartment and parked out front.

"You gonna be okay?" he asked.

Marley nodded. "Thanks for being there for me," she said. "I didn't know who else to call."

"Anytime," he said. "You know that, right?"

Marley nodded. She did know that. She knew that no matter what, she could call on him and he would help her.

"Need me to help you explain all this to your mom?" he asked.

"I'm not actually going to tell my mom," Marley said.

"How can you not tell her?" Hector asked in surprise.

"She's got her own set of problems. Right now, we really, really need the money that I earn from this job. She would feel like I should quit, and then where would we be?"

Hector shook his head slowly. "Were you even tempted when you saw all that money lying around ..." his voice trailed off.

"I was more than tempted," Marley said. "While I was waiting for you? I almost started gathering it up. But I couldn't live with myself if I'd taken the money. I'd be no better than the guy with the bullet in his knee. And Mister

Vimal has been good to me. Besides, it's just plain wrong."

"You're a good one, Marley Macomb," Hector said softly. "Not worrying your mom. Not taking money that was lying on the floor. I don't know too many people like you."

Hector touched her face gently. "Come on," he said. "I'll walk you to the door at least."

Marley was sorry when they reached the door.

"See you Monday," Hector said.

"Thanks again," Marley answered. She opened the door and went inside.

CHAPTER 11

HECTOR

Sunday afternoon, Hector walked over to Ferg Ferguson's house to work on their history project. They had to depict an event that changed the world. Carlos Garcia had suggested 9/11. They wanted to get the project done without much effort. There was so much information and so many photos available on the Internet that they were done in a couple of hours.

"What are Joss and Eva working on?" Hector asked.

"The invention of the telephone," Carlos answered. "They're working on it today. We should meet up with them at Primo's for pizza. What do you guys think?"

"Anybody else working with them?" Hector

asked. He was hoping he'd have a chance to see Marley.

"I think Marley Macomb is part of their group," Ferg answered. "Doesn't she go to Tech too?"

"Yeah, I see her there," Hector said.

"Hey, what happened to you last night?" Carlos asked. "You got that call and then booked."

"Needed to take care of something," Hector said.

"Jacleen break a nail?" Ferg said with a laugh.

"Oh, don't even start with me," Hector said crossly. "And didn't you say something about pizza?"

"Let me call the girls and see what time they want to meet," Carlos said. He pulled out his cell phone and spoke to Joss. She must have asked him something because he turned his back to the others. "Yeah, Ferg and Hector are both here, why?" he asked.

He looked at Hector while he listened to Joss. "Interesting," he said with a grin. "No, of course I won't. Don't worry," he said. "Okay, we'll see you there at four."

He put the phone back in his pocket. "You guys want to shoot some hoops till we meet them?" he asked.

"First I want to know what was so interesting," Hector said.

"Can't say," Carlos answered. "Joss'll kill me. But you're coming to Primo's, right?"

"Yeah, why?" Hector answered.

"Nothing. Just that someone else is going to be there. I think the girls want you to dump Jacleen and find someone new. And they already know who they want that to be."

"Hmm. You're right. That *is* interesting," Hector said, smiling.

"What is?" Ferg asked, frustrated. "What are you talking about?" he said.

"Marley Macomb," Carlos said. "But don't say I told you so."

"Marley Macomb what?" Ferg said. "I'm so confused!"

"Marley Macomb nothing," Hector said. "Let's go play."

CHAPTER 12

MARLEY

Marley was glad she'd called Joss and Eva to say she could come over after all. She was enjoying the Sunday off, and she hadn't thought about financial problems once. She tried not to think about the robbery, but *that* was difficult.

Around three, Joss closed her laptop. "I say we quit working," she said. "I'm fried."

Eva closed her binder. "You won't get an argument from me!" she said. "But I don't feel like going home yet. My house is too crazy. Have you heard from Carlos? I think Ferg said he was going to play some ball with him. Maybe we could all go to Primo's."

"Count me out if you guys are on a date!" Marley said with a laugh.

"Actually, I think some others are there

also," Joss said. "I think Zander Peterson was coming and Durand Butler and Hector Turcio."

Joss raised her eyebrows comically.

"Oh, stop!" Marley said with a laugh. "He's with Jacleen."

"I don't get that," Eva said. "Jacleen hangs out with Brennay Baxter and Zakia Johnson—that crowd. They're certainly not the nicest girls at school. And Hector's a nice guy."

"He's blinded by her looks," Marley said. "Maybe he'll see through her some day."

Joss tilted her head. "Hmm," she said. "Maybe we could help speed things along."

"Really, stop!" Marley said, giving Joss a playful shove. "We're friends. That's all. We're together every day, and we've gotten to be good friends. That's it."

Right then, Joss's phone rang. She read the caller ID and went into another room to answer.

After a few minutes, she came back into the room. "That was Carlos," she said. "He and the guys are going to Primo's around four. I told him we'd meet them there. That okay with you two?"

Marley hoped Hector would come. She didn't

want Joss and Eva to know how she felt, so she didn't ask if he'd be there for sure.

At around four, the girls walked over to H Street. They got the big round table at the back. A few minutes later, Carlos, Ferg, and Hector came in. After a lot of scrambling, they took their seats. Hector sat beside Marley.

"How are you feeling?" he asked, keeping his voice low.

"Still a little shaky," she whispered. "I keep thinking about what might have happened."

"But it didn't," Hector said. He reached over and took her hand under the table. Marley felt like they had a secret no one else at the table knew anything about.

The server took their order. Soon the pizzas arrived, and everyone settled in to eat.

"Let's go to the hill," Joss said after they polished off the last slice. The hill was a spot behind the high school where Cap Central students liked to hang out. It was the highest spot in their neighborhood. From the hill, kids could look out over D.C.

"You want to go?" Hector asked Marley. "Or I can take you home if you're not up for it."

"I guess you should take me home," Marley said. She felt uncomfortable being in a situation that might look like a date. Hector had a girlfriend. She didn't want to cause him problems with Jacleen.

"It might do you good to be with other people," Hector said.

Marley put her hands on her hips and looked at him quizzically. "Don't you think Jacleen might be a little upset by you hanging with me?" she asked. "She doesn't seem to like me much."

"Jacleen who?" Hector said with a smile. "Don't worry. That's over," he added.

"Really? She know that?" Marley asked.

"She will soon enough," Hector said. "Now, hill or home?"

"Hill," Marley answered. She wanted to hang with her friends. Actually, she wanted to hang with Hector.

They sorted out who was riding in Hector's car and who would ride with Joss. Marley ended up in Hector's car.

When they got to the hill, Joss spread out a big blanket she kept in her trunk. The two couples—Eva and Ferg, and Joss and

Carlos—sat on opposite corners of the blanket. That left Hector and Marley in the center.

Below them, they could see the lights of the cars on the streets of D.C. "Seem to you like there's more cars than ever these days?" Ferg asked.

"Yeah, and more and more of them have Maryland and Virginia plates," Hector said. "Now that we're so hip and all."

"Right. So hip that somebody got shot on Benning Road last night," Eva said. "Did you guys hear about that? Hey, were you working at the store last night?" she asked Marley. "Did you see what happened?"

"Yeah, pretty much," Marley said reluctantly.

"And?" Ferg asked.

"A guy tried to rob the Kwik," Marley said. "The cops shot him," she added.

"Whoa, girl! Were you there when it happened?" Carlos asked.

Marley was quiet for a moment. "Yep," she said softly.

Joss gasped. "Tell us," she said gently.

Marley told the story. Her voice was flat. She did not overdramatize what happened or her role in it. Hector put his arms around her and held her close as she talked.

When she was done, everyone was quiet. "I never could be as brave as you," Eva said. "Are you going to go back to work there?"

"Probably," Marley said. "I haven't really thought about that. As for brave, I didn't do anything brave. I just did what the guy said, and then I did what the cops said."

"So did the cops take you home after?" Joss asked. "I hope you didn't have to take a bus!"

"Nah. I got a ride," Marley said, leaning back against Hector.

"So that's where—" Carlos started to say. "Interesting."

"And on that cheerful note, I think I'm ready to call it a night," Marley said. She stood up and brushed off her jeans. "Can you take me home?" she asked Hector.

Hector stood up too. "Let's go," he said.

They said good night to the others and headed for his car.

"What are you going to do about working at the store?" he asked. "I hate that you're there after dark, on that stretch of Benning."

"For now, that's what I've got," Marley said.

They drove in silence to her apartment. When they parked in front, Marley turned toward him. "You need to decide about Jacleen," she said. "You're either with her, or you've told her you're not. None of this in-between stuff. Got it? I'm not that girl."

"What girl?" Hector asked.

"The girl who's with some other girl's boyfriend," she said.

"And if I'm not with Jacleen any more," Hector said, his voice low. "What girl are you then?"

"When that time comes, you can ask me again," Marley said, opening the car door. "Thanks for the ride."

HECTOR

On the following Saturday, Hector got to the garage before Dez Arnold. He was curious about the tool he had seen. He wondered how many more tools he could find that had WW on them.

He opened one of the bay doors. A car was parked in the bay. Hector didn't know what was wrong with it or whether it even needed to be fixed. But he opened the hood anyway. He wanted it to look like he was working on the car. He walked over to the workbench and looked around. The place was a jumble. Tools were everywhere. There was no order to them.

Hector found several wrenches engraved with WW. Others did not have identifying marks. He looked around and found an old toolbox. It was rusty. When he opened it, it was filled with spiderwebs. Nothing else.

He turned it over and knocked it on the bottom to clear it out. Then he took a rag and wiped the inside. He put the tools with Mr. Woodbine's initials into the toolbox. He didn't know what he would do with them. It just made him mad to see the tools that had meant so much to Mr. Woodbine sitting in such a mess. No one even used them. It was as if someone had stolen them only to be mean. He hid the toolbox behind a stack of tires in the corner.

Dez Arnold came in around eleven. He called out to Hector to come into the office. Hector came in, using a rag to wipe off his hands.

"What you been doing?" Dez asked.

"Just straightening the tool area," Hector said. "My teacher at Tech is obsessive about neatness. I guess it's starting to rub off on me."

"That'd be Woody Woodbine, right?" Dez said, shaking his head. "Nothing much changed there, I guess. One of the many things we disagreed on!"

"Yeah?" Hector said noncommittally. He didn't want to give away a hint that he knew Dez had stolen Mr. Woodbine's tools.

"Oh yeah," Dez continued. "Guy had it in for me from the get-go. Nothing I did was ever good enough for him." His voice was bitter.

"So what happened?" Hector asked.

"He pushed me too far," Dez said. "Disrespected me in front of the whole class. I finally had enough."

"What did you do?" Hector asked. He was curious as to whether Dez would admit to stealing Mr. Woodbine's tools.

"Let him know he had messed with the wrong kid," Dez said. "Left one day and never came back. Went back to Ballou and finished up there. Started working with a real mechanic, not some loser who had to teach because he couldn't get a job actually fixing cars."

"You ever see him again?" Hector said.

"He stopped by here one day. Started talking trash. Accused me of this and that. I told him to get his crazy self out of here."

He shook his head, as if to dislodge a bad memory. "Anyway, got another repo job for you today. Interested?"

"For another thousand toward the Lex? Sure!" Hector said.

"Good man!" Dez said. "This one might be a little more … challenging, let's say. Guy hasn't responded to any of my calls. Hasn't made a payment in two months. Time to get tough."

He pulled out an invoice form and wrote on the back. Then he opened the locked key cabinet and pulled out a set of keys.

"Here's the address and plate number," he said, handing over the paper. "Oh, let me write this down. It's a Honda Civic. Silver," he added. "Listen, I know this guy pretty well. He's got a temper on him, so watch your back."

Hector took the paper and the keys. "Barry Farm," he said, reading the address. Barry Farm was a housing development that had been around for a long time. "Park it around back when I bring it in?" he asked.

"You got it," Dez agreed. "Be careful."

Hector nodded. He used his cell phone to figure out the fastest way to get to the address. It wasn't far, so he decided to walk. When he got to the address, he continued walking. He wanted to assess how hard the job was going to be. The few people he saw didn't pay him any attention.

He looped back and pulled the key from his

pocket. He used the remote to open the door. As he put the key in the ignition, something hard knocked against the window. He looked up into the barrel of a handgun.

"Son, you've got about three seconds to get out of this car," the guy holding the gun said.

Hector was so scared. He wasn't sure his legs would support him. He opened the door slowly and got out of the car.

"You just boosting cars in the middle of the afternoon?" the guy asked, still pointing the gun.

"Not ... not boosting it,' Hector stammered. "Dez Arnold gave me the keys. Told me to bring it in."

The man nodded. "Arnold's a hard-hearted son of a ... I'd like to shoot you, but I don't want to mess up my car," he said. "You tell Dez Arnold for me that I'll make things right. He knows I'm good for it. Just going through a rough patch right now. Ask him for a week. I'll make it good by this time next week. You do that for me?"

Hector nodded. He didn't trust himself to speak.

"Now get out of here before I change my mind."

Hector nearly ran up the street. No way could he walk a step more. He got to the bus stop as a bus was pulling up. His heart didn't slow down until he was nearly back to the garage.

Dez was in the office when he got back.

"How'd it go?" he asked.

"Not good," Hector answered. He sat down. He still felt shaky. "Guy came out as I was about to drive away and pointed a gun at my head. Made me get out of the car. Asked me to ask you for another week. Said he'd make it good by this time next week."

Dez's eyes narrowed as he listened. His expression was cold and hard. "Guy's playing me," he said. "Word gets out that I gave him a break? Ain't nobody gonna pay on time. He's got to be schooled. Give me the keys. I'll figure something out."

Hector winced. "I don't have them," he said. "I had already put them in the ignition when he came at me with the gun."

Dez was silent. "Son, you let me down," he said finally. "Them keys all I got to get that car back."

Hector didn't know what to say. He had

never given the keys a thought. He had just wanted to escape with his life.

Dez picked up a piece of paper. He made a line through something. " 'Fraid you're back to zero," he said. "Losing those keys wipes out the thousand you earned last week."

"I'm sorry," Hector said. "Didn't want to get myself killed."

"You arguin' with me, son? You think you deserve something for giving away the only thing I had on this guy?" Dez asked coldly. "You cost me. Big-time. So you're gonna pay. You're lucky that thousand bucks is all I'm charging you. Now get out of here. I don't want to see your loser face for the rest of the day."

Hector got up and left. This was a side of Dez Arnold he hadn't seen before. He knew this was probably what the people who couldn't pay their loans saw. It was as if Dez Arnold's preference was for him to be shot, as long as he got the car back.

Back to ten jobs. That's all he needed to own the car outright. As long as he could stay alive.

MARLEY

Monday morning, Marley got to school and filled out an emergency counseling appointment slip. Those slips guaranteed a meeting with a school counselor on the day they were turned in.

Mrs. Blackwell, the school counselor, called Marley out of first period. Marley asked the counselor if she knew of any programs that could help in a crisis like the one her family was facing. She explained how they'd gotten into this trouble: her mother having the twins, then losing her job when she couldn't find affordable day care for all three younger kids. Mrs. Blackwell listened sympathetically, occasionally taking notes.

"I don't know of any place that can pay your back rent," she said. "I don't want to hold out any hope there. But I can try to call the landlord to see if he'll hold off for a while longer. I can tell him that I'm working with your family to try to solve the problem. Would that help?"

Marley nodded. She knew it was a long shot, but it was better than nothing.

"Meanwhile, how are things going at Tech?" Mrs. Blackwell asked. "I know it must be a difficult schedule."

"It is, but I really like it," Marley said. "I'd hate to have to …"

"Hate to what?" Mrs. Blackwell asked gently.

"Hate to have to give it up," Marley said. "But honestly, I think I may have to drop out of school to work more hours at my job. I'm not seeing many alternatives here."

"Have you asked your boss for more hours?" Mrs. Blackwell asked. "Or if he could even give you more hours if you did drop out?"

"Yeah, I started working later this weekend," Marley said bitterly. "Here's how that worked out." She told Mrs. Blackwell about the shooting.

The counselor shook her head sympathetically. "Bad luck, your second night of later hours. Look, I don't know what can be done here. But let's view dropping out as an absolute last resort, okay?" she said. "Meanwhile, I'll make some calls. I'll get back to you when I have some answers, even if they're not what you want to hear. I promise, okay? And, Marley, don't lose hope," she added.

"Thanks, Mrs. B," Marley said. She left and went back to class.

She had little hope that Mrs. Blackwell could solve her family's problems. Short of winning the lottery, there seemed to be no solution.

HECTOR

On Friday, Hector got a text message from Dez Arnold. "Stop in for a minute this afternoon. Got a job for you."

Hector told Marley he had to go to the garage after class at Tech. He told her she could wait for him in the car. He would drive her home after he talked to Dez, or she could just take a bus.

She rolled her eyes. "Sit outside that place?" she said. "No thanks. I don't ever want to be associated with him. I'll take the bus."

As soon as class was over, he headed for the garage. He walked into Dez Arnold's office and sat down. "You wanted to see me?" he asked.

"Yeah. How you doin'?" Dez asked.

"Okay," Hector answered. He wondered what was coming. He wondered if Dez had decided to make him give back the car. At this point, he didn't even care. He wanted out. It would be a relief.

"Got another job for you," Dez said. "Big one this time. You interested?"

"Depends on what it is," Hector said.

Dez nodded. "That's fair," he said. "Guy last week? Promised to pay by today."

Hector nodded.

"Never heard from him. And his apartment is empty. He seems to have vanished."

Hector couldn't believe it. He'd actually thought the guy would be good for the debt.

"Thing is? One of my boys saw the car parked in a lot off Firth Sterling Avenue, by the Anacostia Freeway," Dez continued. "I think the guy moved and never told me. He needs to be taught a lesson."

Hector didn't like where this was going.

"See, if word gets out that folks can renege on their loans, my business is over," Dez said. "Word needs to be out that I mean what I say. Hear me?"

Hector nodded.

Dez was silent for a moment. "How'd you

like to own that Lexus free and clear by this time tomorrow?"

At one time, Hector knew he would have done almost anything to own the car. But he was learning that there was a limit to what he was willing to do.

"For doing what, exactly?" he asked. He was afraid that Dez wanted him to kill the guy who owned the car.

"For torching the car," Dez said. "Tonight. It's an easy job. You drive over there with a five-gallon gas can in your trunk. You spill the gas around, light a match, and walk away. Nobody gets hurt. Nobody has time to pull a gun. Come in tomorrow, I hand you the paper on that car, and it's yours. Free and clear. Interested?"

Hector knew he should say no. It was wrong. If he got caught, he could go to jail. Something went wrong? He could even die.

He wasn't a guy who set cars on fire. He was a guy who fixed cars.

But the job did sound easy. Low risk. Property damage, obviously, but nobody hurt. He was actually relieved that Dez hadn't asked him to kill the guy.

"You don't want to do it? I can find someone who can," Dez said. "I'm willing to pay big. You know anyone who needs cash?"

Marley.

Marley needed cash, Hector thought. For a moment he considered asking Dez to let Marley do it instead. Then he shook his head. He almost laughed out loud. As if Marley would even consider doing this job! She'd tell him he was out of his mind. And then probably call the cops.

"Nah, I'll do it," he said. "But I want to get this straight. I torch this car, and you'll sign over the title of the Lexus to me. I'll be done—free and clear. No more repo jobs, no more dumping cars to be stolen."

"You'll be done. You'll never have to come around here again, except to pick up the paper on the Lexus. We'll shake hands and move on."

Hector sighed. He knew he was crossing a line from which there was no return. "I'll do it," he said, hating himself as he said it.

"Good man," Dez Arnold said. He pulled out an invoice and wrote the address on the back.

"Here you go," he said, sliding the paper over the desk. "Don't go till after midnight. Less chance of witnesses. Park close enough so you can get out quick, but not too close. You don't want anyone to see your plates. And back the Lex into the bay so you can put the gas can in the trunk. We don't need to advertise what you're up to."

Hector folded the invoice and put it in his shirt pocket. He walked out to the curb and got in his car. There was still time to change his mind. The more involved he got, the harder it would be to walk away. He shrugged his shoulders and decided to think about it later.

He turned on the car and backed into the driveway in front of the bay. He opened the trunk and put the red gas can inside. Nobody else was around. So he retrieved the toolbox he had hidden and put it in the trunk too.

He walked back to the office and told Dez he was leaving.

"Watch your step tonight," the older man said. "But take care of my business. You do this? You'll deserve that car! You'll have earned it, fair and square."

Hector nodded. He didn't want to do this job. But he wanted to own the car.

MARLEY

After class, Marley took the bus to the Kwik n'Carry. She was just about to the store when the phone rang. It was Mrs. Blackwell.

"I wanted to let you know what I've been able to do this week about your family's situation," the counselor said. "Can we talk for a minute now?"

"I'm about to go to work, but I have a few minutes," Marley said. "I hope you found me a rich, dead uncle who decided to leave me his millions."

"Hmm. I'm still working on that," Mrs. Blackwell said with a laugh. "But in the meantime, here's where we're at. Your landlord has agreed to hold off on the eviction. He needs you to come up with a payment plan that includes paying the back rent that you owe and keeping current. He understands that this is going to be hard for you, so he wants to talk to you and your mom about what you can do. I'm not sure what the options are, but at least he has agreed not to start eviction proceedings for at least three months. Can you live with that?"

Marley was elated. "Oh my gosh," she said breathlessly. "That's great. Thank you so much!"

"Marley, I want to be clear. This is only a temporary solution. You need to come up with a more permanent plan, or you're going to be facing eviction again three months from now. Do you understand?"

"What I understand is that we're not going to be living in our car or in a shelter for three more months," Marley said. "Thanks to you."

"Well, and here's the other thing," Mrs. Blackwell said. "I spoke with your mom, and it seems like there are a lot of services your family is eligible for that you're not receiving. I'm sending the school outreach counselor over next week to go over these services with your mom and get her signed up. There are programs out there that can help. She should use everything she can. Sound good?"

Marley couldn't believe it. "Sounds great," she said. "I can't thank you enough."

"Marley, I want to see you achieve your dream. I know how important it is to you that you finish the IT program at Tech. I feel like someday our country will be safer because you're looking for cyberthreats. Anything I can do to keep you on that path is worth it. Now be careful at work, and have a good weekend."

HECTOR

Before going home, Hector turned back toward the Tech campus. The parking lot was almost empty. Mr. Woodbine's car was still there.

He tried the main entrance door, but it was locked. He knocked, but after a while he realized no one would hear him.

Hector walked around the building to the windows of the auto shop room. He looked in. Mr. Woodbine was at his desk working. Hector tapped at a window. Mr. Woodbine looked up. When he saw Hector, he looked surprised. He came over to the window.

"Forget something, Mister Turcio?" he asked.

"I found something of yours," Hector said. "Can you meet me at the back door?"

Mr. Woodbine looked suspicious. "Something

of mine? What on earth could you have found that is mine?"

"Just meet me," Hector said. "Trust me. You're going to like it."

He went back to his car and opened the trunk. As he reached for the toolbox, he again saw the red gas can. Just seeing it made his stomach clench with tension. He slammed down the lid of the trunk and walked over to the door. Mr. Woodbine was holding it open.

"What do you have there?" he asked.

"I think these are yours," Hector said. "Don't know if they're all in there, but I grabbed everything I could find." He handed the toolbox to the teacher.

Mr. Woodbine looked quizzically at him. He set the heavy box down on the floor and opened the lid. Inside were lots of tools. He picked up a hammer and rubbed his finger over the WW engraved on the wooden handle.

"Where'd you find these, son?" he asked softly.

"I'll tell you, but I'll never tell anyone else," Hector said. "I won't testify or talk to the police. If you can live with that, I'll tell you."

"I'm too old to mess with whoever did this to me," Mr. Woodbine said tiredly. "I just want to know."

"Dez Arnold had them," Hector said. "I found them in his garage."

"I knew all along it was Dez," Mr. Woodbine said harshly. "He practically admitted it to me. Wanted me to know what he'd done. What are you doing in his garage?"

"I was working there," Hector said. He didn't even realize he had already put it in the past. "You told us to try to get practical experience. He told me I could work on cars there."

"He actually work on any cars?" Mr. Woodbine asked. "I thought all he did was take them from people who borrowed money from him."

"You know about that?" Hector said.

"Son, everybody knows that," Mr. Woodbine said. "I can't tell you how many times the police have talked to me, trying to get some proof of his illegal dealings. You need to get as far away from him as you can. He's going down. I don't know when, but I know it like I know my own name."

"Well, I'm pretty much done," Hector said.

"Tomorrow's my last day. That's why I wanted to get this back to you tonight."

"I'm glad to have these old friends back," Mr. Woodbine said, shutting the toolbox. "I thank you for this. Now do an old man a favor and promise me you'll have nothing more to do with Dez Arnold. Not even one more day. It's not worth it."

"I'm just about through," Hector said. "The next time you see me, I'll have quit."

Mr. Woodbine looked sad. It was almost as if he knew Hector was going to do something dangerous. He shook his head sadly.

"I'll see you Monday," he said. "Take care."

"I will," Hector said. "And don't you worry about me."

He left the school and headed for Northeast. On the way, he called Jacleen. He asked if he could see her that evening. She said she was getting her hair and nails done. She told him she was hanging out with Brennay Baxter, Zakia Johnson, and some other girls later that night. She asked him to pick her up around nine to drive her to Brennay's apartment.

Hector stopped at home and changed his

clothes. He put on a black T-shirt and dark jeans. He tried to eat, but he was too nervous.

At nine he picked up Jacleen. She got in the car and immediately started talking about her plans for the weekend and all the places she needed him to take her.

"It's not happening, Jacleen," he interrupted. "I'm afraid this is the last ride you're getting. We're done."

Jacleen was so startled she didn't speak for a moment. "What do you mean, 'we're done'?" she asked. "You're breaking up with me? Are you kidding?"

" 'Breaking up'?" Hector repeated with a laugh. "That would mean we had some sort of relationship. I've been your chauffeur, but that's about it," he said. "And now I'm done doing that."

"Seriously? Look at yourself," Jacleen said coldly. "And then look at me. Who do you think should be breaking up with who in this relationship?"

"Whom," Hector corrected her automatically. "But what relationship?" he asked. "There is no relationship! I'm driving you to Brennay's, and then we're done. That's it. Find your own way home. Find your own way from here on. We're over."

"You are such a loser!" Jacleen shouted. "You really think anyone else is ever going to look twice at you? The most you want to do is work on cars! Good luck. Maybe you can find someone who doesn't mind you having grease under your nails, but it's not me."

Hector stayed quiet.

"Wait a minute," Jacleen said. "I know what's going on here! You already *have* found someone who doesn't mind how dirty you look, haven't you? It's Marley Macomb! That b—"

"Careful," Hector said coldly. "You leave everyone else out of this. This is between you and me, and that's all."

"You had your chance, but you are too stupid to take it," Jacleen said tartly. "Breaking up with me? Picking that ugly, rough-looking Marley Macomb over me? Are you *kidding* me? You know she's poor, right? Have you seen where she lives? And what about this car? You're giving it back, aren't you, loser? All these great things are yours, and you are too stupid to hold on to them."

Hector didn't bother to answer. He wasn't going to tell her that after tonight, he would own the car. He was done with her. Marley or no Marley, he couldn't wait to be rid of Jacleen.

He pulled up in front of Brennay Baxter's apartment. Jacleen got out and slammed the door. She stormed off without even saying goodbye.

He felt relieved that he had finally gotten out of a relationship that wasn't at all what it had looked like to others. Now he was free.

He turned the car around and headed back toward New York Avenue.

MARLEY

It had been a slow night at the Kwik n'Carry. But Mr. Vimal had stayed with Marley and Emmitt the whole time. He told them he was going to change his system. From now on, there would be three workers on duty at all times.

At nine forty-five, the door opened. Hector walked in. Marley was surprised to see him. She was also really happy to see him. "What are you doing, shopping on a Friday night?" she said with a laugh.

"Nope," he said. "Thought you could use a ride home."

"Really?" she said. "Thanks! But I still have fifteen minutes."

"You can go now," Mr. Vimal said. "Your replacement will be here in a few minutes."

Marley went into the back and came out with her purse. She walked outside with Hector and got in the Lexus.

"I just wanted to tell you that I broke up with Jacleen," Hector said as he pulled out of the parking lot.

Marley wanted to cheer. Instead, she tried to make her voice sound sympathetic. "How are you feeling?" she asked.

"Pretty fine, actually!" Hector said with a laugh. "We weren't exactly Romeo and Juliet, you know?"

"How did Jacleen take it?" Marley asked.

"She was pretty mad," Hector said. "Accused me of all sorts of stuff."

"Accused you? Of what?" Marley asked with shock.

"Of breaking up with her so I could be with you," Hector said.

Marley was speechless.

"You're not saying anything," Hector said finally. "Not like you to have no reaction."

"But why would Jacleen—I mean, I never— she had no reason to—" Marley sputtered.

"Let's forget about Jacleen, okay?" Hector

said softly, putting his hand on Marley's. "For the first and probably last time in her life, she was actually smarter than she looks."

"Really?" Marley said.

"Really!" Hector answered with a smile.

Marley laced her fingers through his. Her heart soared. First Mrs. Blackwell had delayed her family's eviction. Now this. Marley thought this might just be the best day of her life.

Hector pulled up in front of her apartment. "Can I see you tomorrow?" he asked.

"Sure," Marley said. "I'm working until seven. But I'm free after that."

"Let's grab a pizza at Primo's or something."

"Sounds good," Marley said. "Want to just meet me there?"

"Of course not!" Hector said. "I'll pick you up at the store!"

Marley leaned over and kissed his cheek. "I'm proud of you," she said. "Now if you'd only get rid of this evil car."

She shut the car door. It took a huge effort for her to not dance her way into her apartment.

HECTOR

Hector waited to make sure Marley got into her apartment safely. He could still hear her last words to him. He knew she wouldn't be proud of him if she knew what he was about to do.

By this time tomorrow, he'd be free of Dez Arnold. And the Lexus would be his own. He hoped Marley would never find out what he had to do to get the car. He checked the time on his phone. It was nearly eleven. Dark enough and late enough. There wouldn't be many people around.

Showtime.

He checked his phone for the directions. Then he headed to where the car was parked.

He drove down the street and spotted the car. Right where Dez had said it would be. He passed it and drove around the neighborhood a few times. He pulled in against a curb about a block away. He turned off the Lexus and popped the trunk.

He sat in the car and didn't move.

He really, really didn't want to do this.

He knew it would only take a couple minutes. Then it would be over. But he also knew he'd have trouble living with himself after doing something so wrong. He wasn't this guy.

But he was about to be.

Reluctantly, he got out of the car. He picked up the red gas can from the trunk and slammed it shut. He didn't lock the car. He wanted to be able to get away fast.

He took a rag and wiped down the gas can to make sure there were no fingerprints on it. He checked his pocket for the matches. Then he put on a pair of latex gloves and picked up the can.

He walked slowly back to where he had seen the car parked. He didn't see anyone out in the neighborhood. That stretch of Firth Sterling was deserted.

He got to the car and crouched down just behind the driver's-side door. He pulled the cap off the spout of the gas can. He tipped it over and gas streamed out beneath the car.

"Daddy?" a little voice said from inside.

Hector quit pouring the gas. Suddenly, a child of about three popped his head up and looked right at Hector.

"Daddy, who is that man?" the child asked.

"What man?" a man's voice said sleepily from inside the car. "Go back to sleep."

"What is that man doing?" the little kid said.

"What—hey!" the man shouted as he caught sight of Hector. "What the—"

He threw open his door and jumped out. He was holding a gun out in front of him. It was pointed directly at Hector. With his thumb, he released the safety.

Hector raised one hand. With the other, he slowly put the gas can down.

"Mister, I'm sorry," he said. "Nobody told me there'd be anyone in this car." He raised his other hand so the guy could see both.

He could see a woman now, sitting up in the passenger seat. She was holding a baby.

"You the same guy Dez Arnold sent last week?" the man asked.

"Yeah," Hector said. "He was mad that you didn't pay up. So he told me to torch your car to teach you a lesson. He knew you moved out of your place, but he didn't know you were living in the car."

"That right?" the guy asked. "You sure about that?"

"Nah, I'm not sure of anything anymore," Hector said sadly. "Except that I am done doing anything for Dez Arnold. I could have killed you—you and your family. I am truly sorry," he added.

He lowered his hands. The guy kept the gun pointed at Hector's chest.

"Mister, you need to get out of town," Hector said. "Dez is hot to teach you a lesson as a way of teaching everyone who borrows from him how tough he is. I'm done, but somebody else is going to step into my place. You have to get away."

"To go where?" the man said roughly. "D.C.'s always been my home. Besides, I'm down to my last drop of gas. Sometimes we need it to run the car's heater."

"Take what's in the can," Hector said. "Least I can do. Just don't light any matches.

I started pouring the gas under the car when your boy woke up."

The guy put the gun in his waistband.

"Son, I don't know what Dez Arnold has on you to make you do bad stuff," he said. "But whatever it is, it ain't worth what could have happened here. My boy didn't wake up? You would have had four dead bodies on your conscience. And I'll bet this car that Dez Arnold found a way to hide his role in this. You would have taken the fall on your own."

Hector shook his head in disgust. "Mister, I totally agree with you," he said. "Sooner I get free of him the better." He stuck out his hand. He saw he was still wearing the gloves and took them off. Then he stuck his hand out again. "Good luck to you, sir," he said.

The guy shook his hand. "And to you," he said. "I don't want to read about you in the paper as another dead kid in D.C. Hear me?"

"You won't," Hector said. "I promise you."

The guy nodded and picked up the gas can. He reached in the front seat of his car and popped the gas tank cover. Then he unscrewed the cap and poured the gas into the tank.

Hector watched him. When the can was empty, the guy set it down. "Want it back?" he asked.

"Keep it," Hector said. He gave a small wave to the woman in the car and started walking toward the Lexus.

He knew he would have to face Dez Arnold's anger.

But all he felt was relief.

CHAPTER 20

MARLEY

Marley woke up early Saturday morning. She came out to the kitchen. Her mother was drinking a cup of coffee.

"Mrs. Blackwell told me she spoke to you this week about services," Marley said. "Sounds like there are some things we're eligible for that we aren't taking advantage of."

Her mother nodded. "She was great," she said. "She's sending someone over next week to help me fill out forms. I never applied for programs after the District laid me off because I kept thinking I was only out of work temporarily."

"She said she also got Mister Deane to agree to a three-month break on evicting us," Marley said. "I know it's not much, but it at least buys us time."

"And there's something else too," her mother said. "Remember LaToya Henry who filled in for me when I was out having the twins, and then got my job when I couldn't come back to work? She's pregnant!"

"Uh, I'm happy for her," Marley said, not understanding where her mother was going.

"More than that, she's having some trouble," her mother said. "She's been told she needs total bed rest for the next three months. They asked me to fill in for her!"

"Oh, Mom! That's great!" Marley said. "I mean, I'm sorry for her, of course. But what will you do with the kids?"

"That's one of the things Mrs. Blackwell is going to help me with," her mother said. "In the meantime, Mrs. Jordan from down the hall has agreed to watch them. She has two little ones of her own, and she's home all day anyway."

Marley couldn't believe the news. She threw her arms around her mother and gave her a hug.

"Let's hope LaToya decides not to come back," she said. "Then you can have your job back for good."

"Even if I don't get that job, there are lots

available there that I'll hear about once I'm working again," her mother said. "And once we get on our feet again, I hope you can cut back on your hours. I know how hard you've been working to help out. I want you to start enjoying high school and not have to think about us, hear me?"

Marley nodded happily. "Speaking of school, I need to go to the library this morning to do homework for my IT classes," she said. "As soon as we're paid up on our rent, I really hope we can buy a computer. Even if it's used."

"As soon as we're paid up on our rent, I'm getting my hair done," her mother said with a laugh. "I look a fright!"

"As soon as we're paid up on our rent, I'm getting some new jeans," Marley said. "Mine are so worn out, there are parts you can see through!"

"As soon as we're paid up on our rent, I'm loading up our freezer so I always have something good to cook for dinner."

"And real Lucky Charms!" Marley said.

"Lucky Charms?" her mother said in mock horror. "That's what you've missed?"

Marley laughed happily. "Among other

things," she said. "I think we're going to get through this, Mom," she added. "I feel like everything's turning around."

"I hope you're right, baby," her mother said. "Now go do your work."

"I'm going straight to work from the library," Marley said. "And after work, I'm going for pizza with a friend."

"What friend?" her mother asked sharply.

"Hector Turcio," Marley answered. "The guy I ride to Tech with every day."

"Is this Hector a good boy?" her mother asked.

"The best," Marley said with a grin.

"Then bring him around. Soon," her mother said. "Sounds like I'd better meet him."

Marley kissed her mother and walked to the bus stop. She couldn't wait till seven.

CHAPTER 21

HECTOR

Hector couldn't sleep. He had showered over and over, but he could still smell gasoline in the air. When he thought about how close he had come to doing something terrible, he felt himself get all shaky.

As soon as it was light, he gave up trying to sleep. He went outside and started cleaning out the car. He cleaned out every compartment. He even used a vacuum to pick up the dirt under the floor mats. When he was done, he checked to make sure his SmarTrip card was in his wallet so he could ride the bus home from the garage.

He drove to the garage around ten. He saw Dez Arnold's car out front. He walked straight into the office.

Dez was sitting behind his desk.

"So?" he asked.

"Didn't happen," Hector said.

"Feel like telling me why not?" Dez Arnold asked coldly.

"Because the guy is living in the car!" Hector answered.

Arnold's eyes were cold. "And?" he said.

"And so was his family! There were little kids! I could have killed them all!"

"Didn't realize there were kids in there," Arnold said.

All of a sudden, the truth dawned on Hector. "You knew," he said with contempt. "You knew the guy was living in there. You wanted me to burn him out!"

"Guy should live up to his word," Dez said.

"What about your word to me?" Hector yelled. "No one was supposed to get hurt. Just the car. You played me."

"Son, it's a cold world," Dez said. "You were willing to do anything for a nice set of wheels. I took advantage of that. Business opportunity and all."

"A 'business opportunity'?" Hector said in disbelief. "Lying to me so I would kill four people was you taking advantage of a 'business opportunity'?" Hector was so appalled he could hardly form the words.

He threw the keys to the Lexus on the desk. "You weren't actually ever going to give me this car, were you?" he said.

"Wasn't ever mine to give," Dez said with a laugh. "Guy never actually signed the title over to me. But give away an ES 350 for ten grand? You had to be trippin' if you think I was ever gonna do that!"

Hector turned to leave.

"Son, you're gonna have a fit of conscience, and you're gonna think about dropping a dime on me," Dez called after him. "But before you call nine-one-one, just remember one thing: it's your fingerprints all over every one of those cars you ditched. There's nothing that ties them to me— only to you. It might look to the cops like you were a serial car thief who drove each car for a while and then left it somewhere."

Hector turned to face Dez. "Actually. There is something in each one of those cars that ties it to *you*," he said with a smirk. "Those invoice forms you used as scratch paper when you wrote down the plate numbers and addresses? I hid them in each car I drove for you. Name of your shop on one side, plate number, description of the car, and place to leave it on the other side," Hector said. "In your handwriting. No one's ever going to find those invoices unless I tell them where to look. Oh—and I wore gloves. Every time I touched one of those cars. So no one will ever tie me to those cars."

He started to leave again. "And in case you think you can waste me to keep me from talking? I left proof of this with a couple of people. Anything happens to me, Metro cops are at your door. I'm not dropping a dime on you, but you'd best not even think about coming after me."

He enjoyed seeing the look of shock on Dez's face as he left the repair shop. Not all of what he'd said was true. But some of it was. The satisfying thing was that Dez Arnold would never know what part was true and what part wasn't.

He walked to the end of the block toward the bus stop. Life would be different without a car. But at least he would be able to live with himself again. He wanted to be the person Marley, Mr. Woodbine, and others thought him to be. He wanted to like himself again.

In the distance, he saw the bus approach. He pulled out his phone and texted Marley. "Gave back evil car. All done with Dez Arnold. Taking bus. Gonna have to meet @ Primo's after all. 7:30 okay?"

WANT TO KEEP READING?

Turn the page for a sneak peek at Leslie McGill's next book in the Cap Central series: *The Game*.

ISBN: 978-1-68021-045-3

CHAPTER 1

CECILIA

Cecilia Calhoun opened the door to the locker room. She almost bumped into Remy Stevenson. Remy was standing about three feet from the door. He practically blocked the doorway. The rest of the step team pushed up against Cecilia as they tried to leave.

"Brennay! Your lover is here waiting for you!" Zakia Johnson called out in a singsong voice. Several of the girls laughed. Remy didn't respond. He scanned the crowd of girls leaving the locker room.

Cecilia knew he was looking for Brennay Baxter, captain of Stepperz, the Capital Central High School step team. Remy idolized Brennay. He waited for her every day. Most days, Brennay just told him to go home.

Brennay pushed through the crowd of girls. "There you are, Remy!" she said sweetly. "I'm *so* glad! Did you bring me your Washington Wizards sweatshirt like I asked you to?"

Remy handed over a sweatshirt.

"You ready?" Brennay said to Zakia.

Zakia pulled out her cell phone. "Go for it," she said, holding it out to use the camera.

Brennay put on the sweatshirt. Then she reached up and hugged the tall, skinny boy. "My hero!" she said. Remy looked uncomfortable. He stared at the floor. Zakia snapped a picture with her cell phone.

More points for Lady Bay, Cecilia thought to herself.

Remy was the focus of a game being played online. Someone had started a blog called "Cap Central Chatter." The blog reported school gossip: who had hooked up, fights, complaints about teachers, and other tidbits. The last item in the blog each time was the same: a chart labeled "Remy Points."

Under the chart's title was a list of girls' nick-names. Points were awarded for interactions with Remy Stevenson. Last night's installment had given four points to "Z-Grrrl" for taking Remy's e-reader. The day before, "Lady Bay" had received three points. Remy had put his arm around her.

The blog even listed "official" rules for how the Remy Points would be awarded. All points had to be documented by a picture sent to the blog's moderator. The photos weren't actually published. The moderator—whoever he or she was—awarded the points and updated the total for each name.

So far, Lady Bay was in the lead with thirty-two points. Cecilia assumed that Lady Bay was Brennay. Z Grrrl, who had twenty-eight points, had to be Zakia Johnson, Brennay's best friend and co-captain. Cecilia suspected that Brennay and Zakia wrote the blog, invented the game, and were holding on to all the photos.

Cecilia knew the super-sweet tone Brennay used with Remy was a lie. The whole purpose of the game was to get laughs at Remy's expense. Everyone at Cap Central was in on the joke.

Everyone except Remy Stevenson.

Remy truly believed Brennay when she told him she loved him.

Believed her when she called him her hero.

Thought she meant it when she said he was the step team's good luck charm.

Remy believed everything Brennay said. He didn't hear her insincerity or fawning tone.

Because Remy was autistic.

Cecilia knew people with autism had trouble reading social cues. They had trouble understanding the meaning behind other people's words or expressions.

For the past several years, Cecilia had volunteered at Crossroads, an after-school program for little kids with special needs. Many of the children she worked with were autistic. She enjoyed the work so much that she had already decided to become a special education teacher. She would do anything to protect the children she worked with from bullies.

Yet here at Cap Central, she was a member of a team whose captain was using an autistic boy as the focus of a cruel game. A boy who didn't understand that the girl he idolized was just pretending to like him.

Every time she saw Remy with Brennay, Cecilia vowed she would put a stop to the game.

She knew she should tell a teacher at the school what was happening.

But as captain of Stepperz, Brennay had a lot of prestige. And it seemed like the whole school was in on the game.

Cecilia had moved into the neighborhood near Capital Central over the summer. She still didn't know other students well enough to enlist their support. The girls she knew best were the Stepperz. They went along with anything Brennay suggested. The last thing Cecilia wanted to do was turn in the only girls she'd gotten to know so far.

And she really didn't even know whom she could tell. Mrs. Hess, Capital Central's principal, relied on the Stepperz to entertain at pep rallies, fund-raising kick-offs, and other school events. Her support had to mean that she approved of the team, its activities, and its captains.

Cecilia wished she could come up with a way of making Brennay, Zakia, and the rest of the school understand how wrong the game was. Or even just a way to make it stop. She hated herself for being so weak. By not doing anything to stop the game, she felt like she was no better than those who played it.

She felt helpless.

And angry.

And disgusted.

With herself most of all.

ABOUT THE AUTHOR

Leslie McGill was raised in Pittsburgh. She attended Westminster College (Pa.) and American University in Washington, D.C. She lives in Silver Spring, Maryland, a suburb of Washington, D.C., where she works in a middle school. She lives with her husband, a newspaper editor, and has two adult children.